WOLF R___ __: FIERCE

WOLF RANCH - BOOK 5

RENEE ROSE
VANESSA VALE

WANT FREE RENEE ROSE BOOKS?

Sign up for Renee Rose's newsletter and receive FREE BOOKS. In addition to the free stories, you will also get special pricing, exclusive previews and news of new releases.

https://www.subscribepage.com/alphastemp

GET A FREE VANESSA VALE BOOK!

Join Vanessa's mailing list to be the first to know of new releases, free books, special prices and other author giveaways.

http://freeromanceread.com

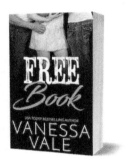

EVI

A *HUMAN* IN THE BUNKHOUSE.

God, this was going to suck.

I'd had my fill of living with humans as a teenager. Being forced to suppress my wolf urges. Hiding my true nature when all I'd wanted to do was run wild and howl at the fucking full moon. Especially with raging teenage hormones. It had practically destroyed me, and the day I turned eighteen, I'd left my human family. Never wanted to live under the same roof as a human again.

Until now.

I took off my hat, rubbed the sweat away with the bandana that had been tucked in my pocket. Clint, Johnny and I had been herding cattle and were finally done for the day.

"It makes no sense." My fellow ranch hand Johnny

hopped down from his horse, dust kicking up around his boots, to close the fence behind us. I leaned against my pommel and waited. "Why have a guy stay here two weeks just to breed a mare?"

And why did he have to stay with us in the bunkhouse? I wanted to ask, but I kept my mouth shut. Everyone already knew how I felt about living under the same roof as a human. About my past trauma.

"It takes, what? A few minutes to pasture mate once they get down to business?" Johnny continued. "It's not like the guy's trying to get some woman pregnant. It's a dang mare."

"I know," Clint let his exasperation show in those two words. "Apparently, pasture mating's too rough for this guy's prized mare. He wants hand mating, and not by us—by his own vet. He's like a... chaperone for a horse."

I snorted.

"I just don't get it." Johnny said. The nuances of horse breeding weren't his thing.

They weren't mine either, really, but if some rich yahoo wanted to have his personal veterinarian babysit a mare he brought to Wolf Ranch to be bred, what did I care? I just didn't like the part where the vet had to stay in the bunkhouse with me and Johnny.

Clint didn't disagree with Johnny. He'd always had a calmness about him, but the fact that he smiled all the time was new. He'd met his mate back in the fall, and they'd had a baby only a few months ago. To say he was happy was an understatement. He was in fucking wolf heaven. A marked mate. A pup.

"It takes more than once to get the job done," Clint reminded us.

"It took you only once," Johnny countered with a sly grin and a wink.

Clint and his human mate Becky had gotten pregnant their first go—a one night stand kind of thing. When he finally figured out she was his mate, he'd moved out of the bunkhouse and now lived in a cabin up in the hills with his new family.

"There are a lot of high maintenance horse people in this country," Clint said. "This guy is one of them. If he wants to have a vet remain to supervise his horse breeding and is willing to pay top price for it, he can waste his money all he wants. We can stand having a human around for a couple weeks. It's worth the money he's paying, believe me."

Johnny frowned although he had no comeback for that.

"Besides," Clint continued. "If his mare can be bred every other day, not just once, the chances of the horse and the vet leaving Wolf Ranch after the two weeks are even better." Clint tipped his hat back. "After that, you'll only have to share the bunk house with this grumpy fuck once again." He thumbed his shoulder in my direction. "Until he's voted in as sheriff in the fall, then he'll be living in my parents' place in town full time."

I climbed down from my horse and led him over to the rail to loosen the bridle. I wanted the sheriff job. It might not lead to justice for my parents, who were killed over fifteen years ago, but I'd get it for others and protect the secret that shifters resided in this county. I'd crashed at Janet and Tom's place a few times when the weather was too bad to drive the canyon road, but living in town? I wasn't so sure about that. The election was months off, so I wasn't going to borrow trouble with arguing about where I was going to sleep.

"He's on his way in," Boyd, our alpha's brother, called.

We stopped our work and looked up. He and his mate Audrey were walking our way from the main house. His pace was slow to match his mate's, who held little Lizzie in her arms. When Audrey wasn't working at the hospital, the three of them weren't far apart. "Fancy truck with a fancier trailer."

I nodded once because it was as I expected. Rich, eccentric horse owner, fancy horse fixins, including a twenty-four/seven vet.

My pack mates might have been happily settled with their human mates, and I liked their mates all right, but humans in general? Not my favorite. Not by a long shot. Marked mates were one thing, but I'd had grandparents who hated the fact I was a shifter... a life that kept my wolf from forever running free. My wolf snarled at the unhappy memory. I still couldn't shift because of my grandparents. I'd been forced to stifle it too much. It wasn't because I was only half shifter. I knew because I sensed my wolf inside of me. He was in there but stuck.

The big truck rolled to a careful stop in front of the stable. Boyd hadn't been kidding about the set-up. This mare, who'd been carefully transported in air conditioned horse trailer splendor, was a pampered princess... was about to get defiled by a Wolf Ranch stallion.

The sun cast a glare on the truck's windows, making me squint. The engine cut off, and a second later, the door opened.

"Oh." Clint stared, eyebrows high enough to get lost beneath his hat.

It wasn't a *guy* who stepped out of the truck—it was a female. And holy hell, she was *all* woman.

"Damn," Johnny whispered, eyeing her with blatant eagerness.

Clint reached out and smacked him upside the head. But I only saw it out of the corner of my eye because I was too busy taking *her* in although I wasn't letting my tongue hang out.

She was tall. I guessed five-ten. Lean, but with curves that couldn't be hidden beneath a pair of jeans. They weren't painted on but hugged her just right. A white blouse was tucked in, the sleeves rolled up and a few buttons undone to show off the long line of her neck. It set off her skin—a warm brown that practically glowed in the sunshine. I realized I'd worked my way up her body because I took in her face last.

Holy fuck, she was gorgeous. Not in the supermodel way, no sir. Her eyes were wide set, nose pert. Lips full and lush. With high cheekbones and a square jaw, she didn't look... dainty. Hell, nothing about her was dainty. Except for the little gold hoops in her ears, the crisp cotton of her top. There wasn't a wrinkle on her. No, not dainty. Fancy, like her truck and trailer.

My dick punched against my jeans, eager to get to her because I hadn't seen a woman that made me instantly hard in a long time. Thankfully, Boyd and Clint weren't getting hard over the sight of her. I shifted my stance to hide that fact and stepped her way.

"Hey, there," Clint said. "I'm guessing you're not Charlie Baker."

She offered him a small smile and tucked her shoulder length hair behind an ear. It was dark brown and smooth, hanging in long layers around her face. My fingers itched to touch it.

What the fuck was wrong with me?

Human. She was a fucking human. Sure, I'd fucked humans before. My dick had gotten hard for them. But not like this. Clearly, it had been too fucking long since I'd gotten off with more than my hand.

"Actually, I *am* Charlie Baker. It's short for Charlotte." Her voice was husky, deep, but held a nervous catch.

Clint tipped his head back and laughed. I stared because it was so new to all of us... that sound. "I'm Clint Tucker. I spoke with your boss on the phone."

"Right. Yes. Nice to meet you," she replied.

"This is Boyd Wolf, his wife Audrey and their little girl, Lizzie."

Boyd took off his hat and ma'am-ed her.

"Another woman on the ranch. Finally," Audrey said. Since Boyd had found his mate in Audrey, the other guys had been dropping like flies. One after the other, each had found a mate, and the sexes on the ranch had been evening out. Especially with two new babies, both female.

"Thanks for having me here at your ranch," she offered politely. Hell if she wasn't a proper thing.

"Well now," Boyd said with his usual swagger. "This is my family's land, but my brother, Rob, runs the place. He's in Billings right now, so you'll meet him later."

"This is Johnny and Levi," Clint offered as an introduction.

We stepped her way.

I took off my hat, nodded. Took a sniff even though my nose wasn't as attuned to scent as a full shifter's. It was annoying as hell, and it made me feel defective. At least I had exceptional shifter hearing. I hadn't been screwed over with that.

After offering Johnny a small smile, then turning her gaze finally on me, her eyes widened. I felt as if I'd been kicked in the chest by a horse. My wolf instantly rose. Howled. Pushed me toward her. Yeah, he thought she was hot, too. Definitely fuckable.

Her eyes narrowed when I moved in close. Too close for a stranger.

She took a small step back.

"Nice to meet you, Charlie." I clasped her hand in mine and energy ran all the way up my arm. A shock of desire. I immediately released her and stepped back, running the affected hand over the back of my neck to alleviate the sensation.

"Well, now that we know you're Charlie but not *Charlie*, we'll get you set up in the main house," Clint said. "I don't think the bunk house will suit."

"I can just stay at a hotel." I couldn't miss the stiffness in her voice.

"Town's twenty miles away. Not all that convenient," Boyd said doubtfully.

Audrey pushed her glasses up her nose and nodded. "Rob and Willow won't mind you staying at the big house."

"I don't want to put anyone out," she said, breaking her gaze from mine and looking to Audrey. "Whatever you originally planned is fine."

"She'll stay in the bunkhouse." I spoke before I even knew I meant to. I usually deferred decisions to Rob or Colton or Boyd, but if I was going to be spending two weeks with a gorgeous female, I wanted her nearby. All my crankiness about sharing a roof with a human was out the window. I'd figured Charlie would be a guy and annoying at that, not a dick-hardening, fuckable woman. This definitely wasn't a bad idea after all.

Clint chuckled. "The bunkhouse is nice and all, but not really meant for ladies. Shared bathroom and all."

"Like I said—"

"She's staying in the bunkhouse," I insisted, cutting her

off and meeting her gaze once more. Holding it. "I'll make sure she's comfortable."

She stared at me but spoke to Clint. "Sounds like this could be difficult. I'll get a hotel room."

Difficult? The only thing that would be difficult would be fitting my hard dick in my pants with her around. I was like an aroused stallion with a mare in heat.

"You'll stay in the bunkhouse," I repeated. "Come on, I'll get your bag."

Her back straightened at my deep tone. I knew it sounded rough, but I couldn't help it.

"Levi, right? I've made things awkward. You all had planned for a man, and then there's me." She set her hand by her neck, and I couldn't miss her short fingernails. Manicured with a pale pink color.

Yeah, I hadn't planned for her. I'd planned on some asshole human male who was going to cramp my style for two weeks. Not a beautiful human vet. And very female.

"Levi, maybe it would be better if she stayed with Rob and Willow," Clint warned.

I wanted to throat punch him. I whipped my head toward Clint and made sure he could see the way I narrowed my eyes.

"I'll stay in the motel," she said. "Sounds like that will be easiest." She was clearly uptight, and I'd made her uncomfortable. Hell, she was like a skittish mare.

I needed to treat her like I treated any nervous filly. I forced myself to relax and stepped forward, loose-limbed and friendly. I gave her my most charming smile—straight out of the Boyd Wolf player's playbook—before he met Audrey, of course. "Definitely not. You're staying in the bunkhouse. With me."

In my bed, preferably.

 HARLIE

I WAS USED to working in a man's world, but there was more testosterone on this ranch than on the entire Bronco football team.

It was nice to see another woman and cute baby, but they didn't do anything to help. Not after Levi had put his foot down.

As I followed Levi to the bunkhouse, I shook off the way they'd stared when I arrived. He'd insisted on carrying all my bags—even wanted to haul my purse, which was ridiculous.

This wasn't the first time time a bunch of horse people had freaked out to discover their vet was a woman. A *black* woman, no less. I'd been busting stereotypes from the beginning in the uppercrust horse world. There was a reason I dressed and acted professionally at all times, even here in Cooper Valley. There was a big difference between Mr. Claymore's spread in Colorado and Wolf Ranch. With my boss, everything was precise and perfect... clinical. He expected perfection in everything from his employees to his horses. That was why I was here in Montana. He wanted his mare bred with a Wolf Ranch stallion to make the perfect offspring. It was my job to see it done. Literally.

Even if it meant staying with a super hot, super sexy, super grumpy cowboy named Levi.

Not that I minded. Not the Levi part but being in Montana. I'd bought myself two weeks of reprieve. The stress of my job. My grandfather starting to be forgetful. Those were nothing in comparison to the blackmail I was dealing with. I popped antacids like they were mints to ease the churn in my gut.

Being here and only having to worry about spreadsheets and horse insemination meant I had my life back. I could— hopefully—forget about ordering more illicit batches of ketamine. I was perpetually freaked that I'd be discovered. I'd be fired. Lose my vet license. Ruined. All because of Dax, an asshole coworker who'd found a way to use me to supply him with his stash to sell.

"Okay back there?" Levi asked, startling me from my thoughts.

I set my hand on my racing heart and glanced at him. He was studying me closely, as if he could read my thoughts. I gave him a fake smile, nodded, then followed.

The bunkhouse was close to the stable, just across a grassy field. Levi led me inside and upstairs to where the rooms opened onto a balcony at one end and a shared bathroom was at the other. We'd cut through a living area downstairs that two other bedrooms opened to. I'd caught sight of a big kitchen and rec room with a ping pong table and foosball. I could see why Clint mentioned it was a space for guys, with simple decor and large furniture for large men. I guessed there were six bedrooms although I wasn't sure how many were occupied.

"You'll be right here." Levi pushed open a door to a plain but clean room with a neatly made single bed, a dresser and nightstand with a reading lamp. He managed my heavy suitcases with total ease, the muscles of his arms flexing impressively as he lifted them onto the bed.

I turned to him, looked him over as he set my stuff down. He was big, with mammoth shoulders and a broad chest. Big enough to make me feel small, and I was plenty tall. Under the cowboy hat, his eyes appeared to be aqua and the bit of hair peeking out looked sandy blond. He had scruff on his face, like he hadn't shaved since yesterday, adding to the rugged cowboy look. He seemed intense yet quiet, which reminded me a little of myself.

Although I wasn't ever called intense. I was *uptight.* Yeah, a woman always wanted to be that. No wonder I was still a dang virgin at thirty. Who wanted to fuck the uptightedness out of a woman? Not Levi, surely. I couldn't imagine he was short of female attention with those roped forearms and sturdy thighs. I had to wonder if he was big all over.

I blinked, surprised by my ridiculous thoughts. I cleared my throat.

"Thank you. Levi, was it?" I asked that, even though I knew his name. I doubted I'd ever forget it.

I stepped back to let him pass, but the room was so small, he ended up brushing close—close enough for me to catch the scent of leather, horse and hay. To see the sheen of sweat on his skin, to know he put in an honest day of hard work and wasn't afraid to get dirty.

Close enough to make my pulse pick up speed at his raw masculinity.

The image of him picking me up and throwing me on the bed slammed into my brain, and I took another quick step backward. God, I was behaving like I was in heat, just like Seraphina. The mare who I'd completely forgotten in the back of the trailer. I wasn't the one here to get fucked.

"Levi, yes." His deep voice seemed to snake underneath my clothes, undressing me with their quiet reverberation as his gaze raked over me. "Sorry if we were awkward back there. You just took us by surprise. We didn't expect the arriving vet to be quite so..."

I arched my brows. "Quite so, what?"

"Beautiful." His face broke into a friendly smile that eased some of the tension in my chest. Despite my resolve to never get involved with anyone at work—even though Cooper Valley was hundreds of miles from work—I found myself more than a little attracted to this giant of a man.

Was it warm in here?

Instead of fanning myself, I rolled my eyes. I wasn't going to fall for his come-on. I wasn't the hook-up with the ranch hand type, especially not five minutes after my arrival.

Sadly, I wasn't the hook-up with *anyone* type. I'd tried it, but... yeah, that hadn't worked out since we hadn't gotten much past first base. Once Levi found out I had a loudly ticking biological clock and that if he wanted to get his dick in me he'd have to punch my V-card, he'd bolt faster than a wild mustang.

Which was fine because I was here to get away from Dax and the crap going down at Mr. Claymore's stables. I hoped being two states away would be a good break from the little shit's threats.

"What's your role here at the ranch?" I asked. I'd spoken to Clint and Rob Wolf by phone and email to organize the breeding visit, but that was all.

"I'm a part-time ranch hand. I do everything from fix broken fences to birth calves." He tips his hat back. "I'm also the acting sheriff of Cooper Valley."

My smile slipped, and my stomach plummeted. "Sheriff?" I whispered then cleared my throat. "You're not wearing a uniform."

He lifted a brow. "Glad you noticed what I'm wearing, doll. I'm not working today."

I could only nod because... *sheriff?* Seriously? The hot guy was a lawman? I was definitely steering clear of this one.

It would be horrible if he found out what I was mixed up in. Knew I was... bad. That I was doing ridiculously illegal things. That the large quantities of ketamine I'd ordered for Dax were probably going to go into the hands of young people. That was what gutted me about this. Sure, he was destroying my life, but I was possibly destroying others by doing what he said. Fuck, my gut churned. I needed another antacid.

"I should see about Seraphina. The horse," I added dumbly. What if Dax got in touch with me? He would. Just because I was away didn't mean the phones didn't work. I took a deep breath, let it out. I'd deal with him when the time came. I was used to startling and jumping at every turn at work, afraid I'd bump into him, or he'd find me alone somewhere. That thought made me inwardly freak.

Hell, what if he showed up here? No. I came to Cooper Valley to get away, to figure out how to get out of the mess I was in. To figure out how to get a guy to stop blackmailing me, all the while somehow staying out of jail.

I just had to play it cool. I had no idea how to do that. I'd been plagued by him for weeks. I hadn't figured out a way to make it stop yet. I was sure "felon" was stamped on my forehead. And with Levi being a sheriff—

"I'm sure Clint and the others are getting her settled in the stable. I promise they'll treat her like a princess."

Okay, he had no idea. *He had no idea.* Breathe!

"Yes, but she's in heat," I finally said, focusing on his words. "She needs to be separated, for now. Then teased in the corral with your stallion. Her vaginal secretions indicate—"

I bit my lip. *Oh my God.* I did *not* just say *vaginal secretions* aloud. In front of this man.

"I'm here to breed a horse," I said finally after taking a breath. Then another. My cheeks were hot, and it was almost impossible to keep my gaze on his, but I forced myself to.

His smile grew, and his face changed from gruff to... gentle. That seemed almost impossible for a guy whose hands were like dinner plates and clearly had DNA of Vikings and cavemen. "Take a few minutes to settle in. I'm sure your boss doesn't expect you to get to work right away. Like you said, the mare needs to be teased first. All females like a little foreplay, right?"

Were we still talking about Seraphina?

His eyes darkened, and I felt like *this* was somehow foreplay for us. Pheromones must be pumping off of him in waves for me to even be all hot and bothered. Speaking of vaginal secretions... my panties were *wet*.

All at once, he stepped back. "Get settled. I'll take care of Seraphina."

When he closed the door behind him, I dropped onto

the bed. What had just happened? That cowboy was interested. In me. I was inexperienced, not an idiot.

He was a *sheriff!*

I needed to keep my distance way more than I needed to get laid by a hot cowboy. Pulling my phone from my purse, I texted Mrs. Vasquez, the neighbor, who was keeping an eye on Pops while I was away. He had signs of early dementia, on occasion forgetting where he was, my name. So far, he was safe, but I worried that might change. I didn't want him to go for a walk and forget where he was or go to take a bath and forget, leaving the water running and flooding the house.

Keeping my veterinarian's license and my job was paramount. With Pops' medical bills and prescriptions on top of the mortgage and everything else, the bigger paycheck working for Mr. Claymore versus buying into a private practice was a requirement.

Now I was stuck. I had to keep my job, so I could order the ketamine for Dax. I couldn't do it if I worked at a regular practice. On a horse farm? Orders would go unnoticed. At least I hoped.

I was screwed. So screwed.

But at least Mrs. Vasquez offered to keep an eye on Pops, so I could be away. He was safe. He had no clue about my troubles or stress. The only perk of memory loss.

Sighing, I let my thumbs fly on the cell phone screen.

Me: How's Pops doing?

She wrote back right away.

Tina: Good. He had dinner at the Elks Lodge. Now we're watching his shows.

I sighed in relief.

Me: Great. Just wanted you to know I made it fine.

Tina: Don't worry while you're there. Have fun!

Don't worry? I had a blackmailer probably wondering where I went.

Have fun? Did she mean with Levi?

Not happening. I grabbed my charger and plugged my phone in. I was here for a job and to figure out how to ditch a blackmailer while doing it. I just had to remember that Seraphina was the one to get thoroughly fucked, not me.

3

EVI

I WALKED INTO THE STABLE, thinking of Charlie with every step.

It was unusual for me to be this attracted to a female. Unusual enough to make me wonder...

No. No fucking way. I would've known if she were my mate. At least, I thought I would. I didn't get that instant recognition thing male shifters said they felt the moment they caught their mate's scent. Like Boyd with Audrey. Colton with Marina.

Of course, my wolf was latent—he was inside me but couldn't come out—so it was possible I wouldn't know.

This was why I wanted a she-wolf for a mate. If Charlie were a shifter, *she* would know if we were mates. She'd tell me. Because my wolf had been broken—whatever the fuck the word was—by my grandparents, I was left playing guesswork. It would be easy if Charlie knew she was mine. Obvious. We'd be fucking right now, and I'd be making her mine. She'd have no doubt she belonged to me, that my mark belonged on her dark skin. It would be as simple as that.

But no. It was possible I was as helpless as any ordinary human trying to figure out "the one."

Fate was fucked up. With my mother being human, I had her DNA, too. Human DNA that kept me from important shifter things. Letting my wolf out. Scenting my mate. Knowing her. More.

As for Charlie? I wanted her. There was no denying it. The chemistry was there if not the mating scent. I growled in frustration. I would have her. I had two weeks to do so.

I stalked into the cool stable, pointed at Johnny who was brushing down my horse. I should thank him for it, but I had more important things to say.

"You're staying with your parents."

"I am?" Johnny asked, eyes widening, pausing with the curry comb on the horse's flank. He might be young, but that didn't mean he wanted to be back at home in his childhood bed. Too fucking bad.

Clint and Boyd were brushing the other two horses down and stopped when I piped up.

"Why's that?" Clint asked, brush in hand. The corner of his mouth was tipped up.

I narrowed my eyes, set my hands on my hips.

"Yes, Levi," Audrey drawled.

I spun about at her voice, not realizing she was in the corner out of the way. She was settled into a chair Boyd must have brought out of the stable office for her. She had a cloth tossed over her shoulder with Lizzie nursing beneath it. I saw her tiny bare feet sticking out from the edge of the pink cover.

A woman nursing a child didn't do a thing for me, not any more than a woman brushing her teeth or eating corn on the cob. But Audrey feeding her infant all of a sudden struck a nerve. I wanted my child suckling at my mate's breast. I envisioned Charlie feeding our baby, and... fuck me. Babies? I was in epic trouble here. *She was not my mate. She did not want my babies. Hell, she didn't even want to stay down the hall from me.*

"Why is Johnny staying with his parents and not in the bunkhouse with you and the lovely veterinarian?" she asked, breaking me out of my thoughts. Her mouth turned up in a sly smile. Those glasses might give her an innocent look, but she was far from it right now.

I wasn't going to snap at Audrey. My wolf might be ready to snarl, but she didn't deserve it, even if she was taunting me. Boyd would also rip my throat out.

"Because I want her," I replied through gritted teeth.

"She's your mate?" she asked.

I crossed my arms over my chest. "No. I don't think so."

"Maybe she is, and you just can't smell it," Audrey countered.

It was possible, but I felt like I'd *know*. It was fucking unfair. A wolf inside me but couldn't be let out to run. Couldn't scent his own mate.

"I want her. That's enough."

Clint slapped Boyd on his shoulder, making me turn and face them. "Twenty bucks, dude," Clint ordered.

"What did you two assholes bet?"

Boyd grinned. "Bet you'd claim her. Wolf or not."

"A tip, Levi," Audrey said, rolling her eyes at her husband and brother-in-law. "*Be nice.*"

I gave her a glare over my shoulder, but she just smiled back.

"Yeah, being a grumpy fucker's not going to help you," Boyd said, pulling out his wallet from his back pocket.

"I'm not grumpy." I took my hat off, ran my hand through my hair.

All of them laughed, and I wasn't sure who to throat punch first.

"Where's her mare?" I asked, trying to redirect, so I didn't start a shifter brawl in front of the horses. The animals had gotten used to us all being shifters, having predators inside us, but we had to be cautious around them. Especially new ones like the horse Charlie brought.

Clint tipped his head. "Put her in the near pasture."

Was it strange that I didn't even like the other guys handling Charlie's mare?

Not just strange, downright nuts. Especially considering Seraphina wasn't even Charlie's. The mare belonged to her boss, Mr. Claymore. Some eccentric millionaire.

Whatever. He could be as eccentric as he wanted because his craziness was what had brought Charlie here. I owed the man a thank you card. And a resignation letter for his soon-to-be former vet because while everything in me resisted wanting a human, I wanted Charlie here, and I had a feeling two weeks wasn't going to be enough.

I turned on my heel and headed out to the pasture, only because I couldn't very well go back into the bunkhouse and wait outside Charlie's room like a crazy stalker. Being with the horse was the next best thing. Like getting to know Charlie's horse—making friends with Seraphina—would somehow get me closer to her prickly veterinarian.

4

CHARLIE

OH, sweet baby Jesus. I should've packed my vibrator. I woke up from the most sexual nap-dream I've ever had. I wasn't sure if I should rub my eyes or my clit.

In the dream, I'd been in this same bed, only Levi, the giant cowboy, had been in here with me.

Looming over me on his hands and knees, framing me in, so all I could see, all I could feel, was him.

Calling me beautiful and—oh my God, what had he said?

It's my job to see to your every need at Wolf Ranch. And it starts with this...

It was only a dream. *Only a dream.*

I didn't even know how I'd fallen asleep! I'd meant to sit down and review the data of all breeding activity for Mr. Claymore's mares over the past eight years, to update the ovulation chart for Seraphina, but the drive from Colorado had exhausted me. Obviously, I'd conked out.

And had a sex dream. Now I was rested but flustered. Horny, too.

For one specific cowboy who was going to be sleeping just down the hall.

I checked my watch as I ran my hand over my hair. Seven o'clock already. I needed to unhook the horse trailer and drive into town to scrounge up some dinner. Damn, how far did Boyd say town was? Twenty miles? My stomach rumbled.

Maybe I would just eat the granola bar in my bag.

I grabbed it off the floor, found my cell. My heart skipped a beat when I saw the text.

Dax: Where the fuck R U? Looking for the vitamin K.

Shit. I took a deep breath, tried to calm my racing heart over the fact he was trying to find the ketamine I'd ordered for him last week. Tried not to throw up. With trembling fingers, I typed back.

Me: It's being shipped.

Dax: U said it wld B here 2 days ago.

Me: I have no control over a shipping company.

That was the truth. I ordered the stuff. How long it took to arrive was not my problem regardless of what Dax thought.

Dax: It had better be.

I sucked in my breath.

Me: What do you want me to do?

Dax: Order more. Get the fast shipping.

Me: I can't order more and send it to the Claymore stables. Too much to one address.

If someone else received the order while I was gone, one

batch might not raise an eyebrow, but two? That was more ketamine than I could explain away.

Dax: Ship the shit there to bumfuck Montana. Bring it back with you.

Ship it to Wolf Ranch? I glanced around. This was insane. Not only did the people here have nothing to do with my shit, but it added more danger. How could I explain away a shipment being delivered? It wasn't like I was on vacation or something. I wasn't ordering a dress online for a wedding. What the hell could I say to Clint about getting mail?

That didn't even take into account that Levi was not only a ranch hand here at Wolf Ranch but also the flipping county sheriff. I had no doubt he could sniff out illegal activity.

Dax: Show me the order confirmation, or I'll go to the vet board.

I felt like puking. If Dax went to the board, I'd lose my license and my job. But at the same time, I definitely couldn't keep this up. I knew it wouldn't stop. He would be pushing me forever. I'd hoped to get some clarity while I was here in Montana on what to do, but I was more freaked out than ever. Being away made it even worse. Made *Dax* even worse.

I didn't wait, just did as Dax wanted. I grabbed my laptop. It took ten minutes, but the order was placed. It wouldn't be here overnight, but it was supposed to arrive before I was supposed to leave.

Me: Done. I attached the screenshot of the order.

A light knock sounded at my door, and I jumped a foot, slapped the lid down on the laptop. My cell clattered to the floor. "Fuck."

I threw the door open, breathless, only to find the subject of my sex dream looming large in the doorway.

Levi's white T-shirt stretched taut around his muscles, his pecs clearly defined underneath the thin fabric. The cowboy hat was gone, and he must've been freshly showered because his square jaw was shaved smooth, and he smelled like soap and rain. In his hand, he held a plate covered in foil.

"Hey," he rumbled, his deep voice slipping into my panties like a dark invitation. "I came earlier to take you to dinner at the main house with the others and saw you were sleeping. I wanted to let you rest but figured you might be hungry now."

"I am!" I didn't mean to sound so eager, but now that the smell of the food reached my stomach, I was starved. And I felt as if he could tell exactly what I'd been up to. I practically snatched the plate from his hand, but he held it up high, out of my reach.

I stilled, confused as to why he offered then yanked it away.

He shook his head slowly. "Uh uh. There's a price, Doctor."

For a split second, I panicked. A price? Was he trying to blackmail me, too? Then I saw the sly twist to his lips, the humor glinting in his eyes. He was playing.

I put my hands on my hips, sighed in relief. Compared to the asshole punk who was ruling my life right now, Levi was a relief. Friendly. Gruff, sure. But I felt safe with him. As if there was a connection or something between us. *More.*

Which, of course, there wasn't, which meant I was delirious from low blood sugar or something.

I couldn't date Levi, though. Fuck, that was my problem right there. I was here for two weeks. There was no *dating.*

He was the sheriff. Acting sheriff, whatever that meant in this town. He was the *law*. I was the proverbial *outlaw*. I couldn't take care of Pops if I lost my license or was in jail.

But right now, he wasn't the sheriff but a guy who was thoughtfully bringing me dinner. I needed to stop reading into everything.

"Whoa, there. Where'd you go?"

I blinked, realized I'd been in my head again. Smiled.

"What's your price, big man?" Oops. That came out way more flirty than I intended. I wasn't sure I've ever flirted before in my life. Never so blatantly.

"Mmm." He backed up, still holding the food out of reach. I was tall, but he had several inches on me. The only way I was going to get that plate was to climb him like a monkey. While that idea sounded appealing, it probably wasn't the best thing to do. "For one thing, you should *definitely* call me big man again." He winked and turned down the hall. "Trust me, I'm big all over."

Oh lord. He *had* taken it as flirting. Why were my nipples getting hard? Was my mind really thinking about how big he was in other places. If the size of his hands were any indication...

I followed him and the plate of food, as he'd surely intended.

"And the other thing?" I asked, eyeing how well his jeans molded to his butt.

"You gotta sit with me." He tipped his head, friendly-like, in the direction of the living-slash-game room.

I arched a brow. "*Sit* with you?"

Ordinarily I wouldn't need to clarify, but I wasn't sure if he meant sit *with* him or sit *on* him. I knew which one I'd rather do.

He smirked. "Or you can do other things. Your choice."

Holy shit, I'd been right.

I rolled my eyes and smacked his arm. I didn't know when I started smacking guys so playfully, nor how he managed to make me feel comfortable enough to do it, but honestly? It felt good. So had the hard muscle beneath my palm.

I'd been keeping myself closed off from men for way too long, as my best friend Keely always told me. Now, with my Dax situation, I couldn't even think about it.

Except I was.

The Cooper Valley sheriff was all but inviting me to sit on his flipping lap, and I was actually considering it.

Except I had no game. No experience. Was way too up in my head when it came to guys. Instead of going with it, I wondered how I got from professional, clothes-on, respectability to naked and horizontal with this guy? Sure, I'd felt up his forearm, but what happened next? I just couldn't picture the steps in between or Levi doing them with me.

He looked at me with heat. Interest. I was smart enough to recognize the signs.

Maybe I could do this. Flirt. Have fun. *Get laid.*

It started like this. Right? My belly suddenly fluttered. Oh, damn. What was I doing?

No law enforcement officers. Shit.

He'd know, somehow, what I was doing. I might have driven five hundred miles, but Dax had already proven he'd keep bothering me here. And if Levi found out I was ordering drugs under the premise of them being for Mr. Claymore's horses but were really being given to Dax?

Handcuffs and not for sexy times.

"I swear I can see your mind working overtime." He studied me. "No wonder you needed a nap."

He was joking, but it stung. He was right. My mind never shut down, especially freaking over the mess I was in.

"Hey, there." He lifted my chin with a finger, so I met his eyes. I didn't see anything but concern. Understanding. "That smart brain of yours works all the time, huh?"

I nodded.

"Well, how about you take a little mental break? Seraphina's all settled for the night. I checked on her myself. There's nothing for you to do but have dinner with me."

If he only knew. No! He could never know. Still, he was being kind. Thoughtful. Gentle. And it was true, the horse was settled, and there really wasn't anything I could do tonight, even for Dax. With a few words, he'd smoothed it over and made me feel better. Maybe it was the soft tone of his voice. Somehow it was soothing. He didn't make me feel bad for being in my head all the time.

"Like a date?" I picked the light banter back up. The direction we were headed had been too revealing.

He grinned and turned away to head downstairs.

I followed him into the living area, where he plunked down on a couch and patted the spot beside him.

"Yup, a date. Just the two of us over dinner."

I laughed because this wasn't a romantic candlelit dinner for two in a fancy restaurant. This was the two of us on a couch with a covered dish.

I settled beside him, just far enough apart so our thighs didn't touch.

"There's my girl. See? That wasn't so hard." He gave me a wink. My heart fluttered at how he called me his girl, but he ruined it all by adding, "But the offer for sitting on my lap still stands."

I gave him the primmest of looks. "I'll have to decline that offer, generous though it may be."

I held out my hand for the plate of food, and he unwrapped it and gave it to me.

"Oh, it's generous," he said, and my body heated at the blatant innuendo.

He then got serious about seeing me fed. "Hope you like burgers. If not, I put a little of everything on there for you." He produced silverware wrapped in a cloth napkin from his back pocket. It was true, the plate was piled high with food —fresh salad, a burger, a slice of watermelon, and scalloped potatoes. "Marina made those buns fresh today. They're to die for."

"Marina?" I asked before taking a giant bite of the burger.

"Oh sorry. She's Audrey's sister. Believe it or not, she married Boyd's brother, Colton."

"That's crazy," I said, mouth full. It was delicious, and I was shoveling it in like a growing teenage boy, which was another thing I didn't usually do in front of people I didn't know. I had better manners than this, but Levi didn't seem to mind.

He reached out, swiped a little ketchup from the corner of my mouth.

I stared at his mouth as he sucked the tip of his thumb. *Oh my.*

I didn't remember feeling so attracted to a guy before. Maybe it was because I felt strangely comfortable with him. I barely knew him. Why was there this... feeling between us? It was weird and thrilling and a little exciting.

This wasn't the hang-out-with-friends comfortable.

No. I didn't think I'd ever consider this big guy with the gorgeous eyes and the potent personality as a *friend.*

A huge zing of sexual attraction ensured the flutters were ever-present. My nerve-endings were alight, even scarfing down a hamburger. It was disconcerting to be so wrapped up in this man's attention. Maybe it was the sexy dream I'd had that was bleeding over into being awake. With him.

No. He was just hot. Attentive. Considerate. Gorgeous.

And a lawman.

I demolished the burger and moved onto the salad with the plate settled on my lap. "How many people live on the ranch?" I asked because I'd already met too many to remember. "How big is it?"

He shifted, settled back further into the couch, as if he had no intention of going anywhere. "Rob and Colton live in the main house with their wives. As I said, Colton's married to Marina. Rob's wife is Willow. I think Colton's going to build another house on the property sometime soon, like Boyd and Audrey have. Clint—the guy you've been chatting with about the breeding—his family has a place up on the mountain, but he used to live here with us before he mat— married. His wife's Becky, and they had a baby in April."

"Yes, he told me about Lily."

Levi nodded. "It's just me and Johnny left here in the bunkhouse."

"I figured the sheriff would stay in town."

He ran a finger over his lips. "I'm *acting* sheriff. The previous one had a heart attack recently."

"Oh no," I said. "Is he okay now?"

"He's fine. He was shoveling snow when he got chest pains. His wife had been on him to retire somewhere warm for years now. That did it. He resigned, and I was voted by the city council to replace him until the next election."

"You have past experience?" I needed to know what kind of background I was facing.

"Nothing like Willow, Rob's wife. She's former DEA."

Oh. My. God. My stomach flip-flopped.

"Willow?" The hamburger felt like a brick in my stomach. There was a DEA agent living in the main house?

"She'd make a good sheriff although she's pretty content here on the ranch. I was a deputy, actually, before. Part time. There wasn't one from this side of the canyon, and it's good to have resources in all areas since the county's so big. Back to your original question, I've lived here for years. Sometimes other ranch hands will stay in the bunkhouse. Rand, who is Clint's brother. Nash. Or guests like you."

"I'm not going to remember any of those names," I admitted. Well, I'd remember Willow's, that was for sure. Holy shit, I was staying on a ranch with the county sheriff and a former DEA agent. And now mail service was going to drop a box of ketamine on their doorstep. This was a big freaking problem.

Levi spoke of them as if they were family. If I had it right in my head, most of them *were* related, but others were accepted and included, like Levi. They were all... *good.*

"Only one name you need to remember," he murmured.

I slapped his thigh and gave him a knowing look. "Let me guess. Yours?"

His hand settled atop mine on his thigh, not letting it move. His quad was like concrete beneath my palm. Rock hard.

"That's right, Doc."

"And why is that?" I whispered, looking up at him through my lashes.

"Because I am your personal host. Anything you need, just ask. I'll take care of you."

It's my job to make you comfortable at Wolf Ranch. And it starts like this...

Oh God. I pressed my inner thighs together to alleviate

the slow burn his presence produced. That his words, the *suggestion* of what he was offering, made me feel.

His gaze tracked the movement. The corners of his lips turned up with a satisfied smirk.

He couldn't possibly know I was horny right now, could he? Why did he look like he did?

Damn his size and rugged cowboy good looks. His dark manly scent. The eyes that seemed to see past every barrier I'd raised over the years. I hadn't known I'd be so susceptible to virile ranch hands.

"I need a shower," I blurted, setting my plate down. Because I did. Not just to freshen up but because of this pulsing between my legs. The need I had for this guy. He was so close. I could reach out and grab him, pull him in for a kiss. Climb onto his lap, straddle his thighs and take a cowboy for a ride. There were so many things I could do, but I just didn't know how to go about it. *Kiss him, Charlie!*

No. I'd die of mortification if he wasn't into it. I had to stay here for the duration of the breeding process, and I couldn't live with myself if I screwed up. And I definitely couldn't let him in my bed where he might learn too many of my secrets.

Frustrated, I stood. I'd never needed one of those massaging showerheads so badly before. I sure hoped they had one here.

His grin widened, showing a row of perfectly white, straight teeth. If it weren't for his size and initial gruffness, I would've called him All-American. But no, underneath the good looks was something a little grittier. A little more dangerous. Animalistic. Fierce, even. He played at casual, but something made me feel like there was more afoot here than flirtation.

He didn't seem like a player to me. He seemed more like

a loner. He might have a pseudo-family here on the ranch, but he was still alone.

Same with me. I had Pops. My co-workers, colleagues. Friends. Besties, even. But I still felt alone. Especially since I couldn't share the biggest secret of all with any of them.

So what was Levi's interest in me? A wild romp with the visiting vet? He was a guy. Of course, that was his plan.

"I can *definitely* help you with a shower," he said, and I cursed the heat that flushed up my neck. Yeah, wild romp.

"No help needed." I jumped to my feet. "I'll, um, just help myself."

Oh *God*. Had I really just said that?

Please let him misunderstand me. Please, God. When I heard his laugh as I bolted up the steps, I knew he hadn't.

5

EVI

CHARLIE WAS NAKED. Just on the other side of the door.

If I'd had any decency at all, I would've gone to my room and shut the door. Given her some privacy. Instead, I stood in the hallway imagining exactly what she looked like with water running over that beautiful dark skin of hers. I wanted to lick the droplets off her nipples. Would they be big or small? Her breasts were on the small side—perfectly sized to cup in my palms, of course—but what was the diameter of her actual nipples?

Why was it so fucking important that I know?

Why was a stupid question.

Because I wanted to know every damn fact about her. Not wanted, *needed*.

I needed to learn where every freckle rested, memorize every dimple, crevice, fold. I couldn't wait to get her on her back moaning my name as she came and came and came again. Back? Hell, up against the wall, bent over the arm of the couch, even in one of the horse stalls.

It was my job. Bringing her to pleasure was definitely *my job*.

She'd come, just as she was right now. Naked, wet. Just on the other side of the fucking door. Yeah, I knew exactly what she was doing.

My keen shifter hearing picked up the sound of the water splashing around her body, but it also heard the catch of her breath, the irregular panting, the intermittent soft moans. When she'd said she'd take care of her needs in the shower by herself, she'd meant it. She was using that fucking showerhead to get herself off right now.

I envisioned her legs parted, the spray hitting those dark folds just right so her clit was hard. I'd bet my left nut it was so swollen the hood was pulled back. The thrum of the spray must be getting her hot, getting her close to coming. My mouth watered to take over, to suck and nibble at that little pearl, to feel her fingers tangle in my hair as I made her come. Made her knees weak. Her breath catch.

Fuck me.

A muffled cry and then—shit... fuck... holy fucking fuck —*my name*, came through the door. I had to reach into my jeans and squeeze the head of my dick, so I didn't come right there in my pants because she was thinking of *me* as she orgasmed. I dropped my forehead against the door as I tried to catch my breath, but all I picked up was her scent along with the soap I used. The combination made me growl.

Thank fuck the water was still running.

It stopped soon enough though, then I was thinking of

her drying off, that soft towel running over every inch of her skin.

I set my palm flat on the door. "Charlie," I said.

The quick inhale couldn't be missed.

"I'll be out in a minute," she called, as if I wanted to get in there to take a piss.

"Was it enough, doll?"

She was quiet for a minute as I stared at the painted wood right in front of my eyes.

"Wh-what?"

"That little bit of pleasure you got. I bet it wasn't enough. I can help with that. I can help you wring it all out."

She gasped then was silent. And silent. I had to turn my head to even hear her breathing.

"You okay in there?" I asked. My dick punched against my jeans, eager to get to her.

"I'm... I can't come out. Not with you there. Not well, ever."

I grinned at the door. I love that I got her all flustered.

"I'll walk away. This time," I added. "Don't be ashamed, doll. You never have to hide anything. Not from me."

I pushed off the door and went to my room, closing the door loud enough, so she knew where I was, that I'd given her room. Just as I said, I walked away. My wolf was pissed, which was odd, but I did it. *This time.*

 HARLIE

"WE'LL LET them be for now," Clint said. "Whenever you want, we can do an ultrasound and check follicle growth."

He was walking with me up the hill to the main house for breakfast. The sun had been up for an hour, but it was still early. Still cool. Dew coated the grass.

We'd met at the stable at five-thirty to do the first hand breeding of Seraphina and Eddison, their prized stallion. It had taken less than an hour, and everything had gone as expected. Seraphina was in the pasture grazing, which was like a post-sex cigarette for horses. Eddison was back in his stall, getting some extra grain for his hard work.

"I'll do it later today and again tomorrow," I replied. "I have a spreadsheet."

He arched a brow, so I continued.

"You talked to my boss."

"I did."

"He's... particular. Likes things done a certain way. Likes data and daily updates. I think that's why I like working for him. I like data, too. It's important to monitor follicular growth, and keeping good records on the mare's specific history is important. It can indicate... well, you know what it can indicate."

I sighed, realizing I was probably oversharing. Clint wasn't just a hick cowboy. He was building a quality stud program here and knew his stuff.

"I like to see horses well cared for," he replied. "As you said, Claymore might be eccentric, but he knows Wolf Ranch has a worthy stallion in Eddison."

I couldn't help but smile. "Yes, we did research on that as well. My job's more than data. He's got twenty horses and is trying his hand at sheep. The trainers and other staff report to me with any issues, and I have to oversee them all. Even from here."

"You specialize in big animal medicine?"

"In my job, yes. Mr. Claymore has a black lab who comes to me for shots, but otherwise, it's all big animals there. I also volunteer at the local animal shelter and spay and neuter dogs and cats once a month."

"You keep busy. It's good to see. No one can be lazy on a ranch like this."

I took in the land around us. Open fields in all directions until they butted up to the mountains. Tall grass, big skies. It was beautiful. The ranch was well maintained, and it showed. I could live in a place like this. While Mr. Claymore's ranch was expansive and tucked back up in the foothills, it was close to Denver. It would be considered practically suburban, while here... it was rural through and through.

No rush hour. No commuting.

"My life got a little crazier this year," he continued. "I lived in the bunkhouse until the fall."

"I heard you and your wife had a baby. Congratulations," I said, smiling, imagining this big guy holding a tiny infant.

Clint grinned. "Thanks. Those of us staying in the bunkhouse usually eat dinner at the main house with the others, family style, but breakfast and lunch is a catch all since everyone's doing different things. As a guest, Marina's expecting you to pop in for all your meals, but you're welcome to grab some stuff at the store if you want to eat on your own or if you've got some kind of food allergy. I can take you into town or tell you where to go."

"I don't want to make extra work for Marina."

He laughed. "Just wait."

He didn't say more as we went to the back and went in without knocking. The screen door slapped shut behind us. The scent of yeasty bread and coffee made my stomach rumble.

"Hey, Marina. This is Charlie." Clint took his hat off, setting it on the counter and making his way to the coffee pot.

The petite woman looked up from her bread kneading on the center island of the huge eat-in kitchen. The space was dated, but homey and lived in. Based on the amount of dough in front of her, she spent a lot of time in here. And fed a lot of people. With the dining table large enough to seat at least ten, it was clearly the central meeting spot of the ranch.

She had long dark hair pulled back into a bun, a black t-shirt dotted with flour and a pair of cut-off jean shorts. "I wondered when you were going to get hungry."

"Thanks so much for the plate last night. I'm sorry I slept

through the meal." I told her. I'd thanked Levi, but he was the delivery guy, not the cook. "It was delicious."

Clint held his to-go mug up. "I'm set. Thanks," he said to Marina then looked to me. "I ate at the cabin before I left this morning. Lily was up early for a feeding, so I had breakfast with my girls. This extra shot of caffeine will do the trick though. You good from here?"

Nodding, I said, "Yes, thanks. I've got plenty of work to keep me busy." My cell chimed, indicating a text, and I laughed. "See?"

Clint nodded, gave Marina's shoulder a squeeze and left the way we came in.

"I've got cinnamon rolls in the warming drawer. If that's not your thing, I can make you some eggs."

I held up my hand. "You had me at cinnamon rolls."

She laughed. "Grab some coffee. Mugs are in the cabinet above the pot."

I stayed out of her way as she efficiently moved about, setting a sticky, glaze-covered bun onto a plate and setting it at the far end of the counter where there were two stools. She set a fork and napkin beside it. "Milk or sugar?"

I sat down then took a sip of the coffee. "Black's fine. Thanks."

I ate in silence as she finished kneading the dough, cut it into equal pieces and placed them into loaf pans.

"If this is breakfast every morning, I'm in big trouble."

"Usually it's eggs of some kind. Something that can sit in the warmer. The guys come in over a stretch of a few hours, so I like to have something ready. Lunch in the summer is sandwich fixings that I lay out for everyone to make their own. As you might have guessed, I love to cook. I'm starting up my own baking business, but I keep everyone around here pretty much fed. At least part time. It's too nice out for me to be cooped in the kitchen all day."

I glanced out the back windows, the view spectacular. It was going to be a warm one but not as hot as in Colorado. "I'd want to be outside, too."

I washed down the sticky goodness with another sip of the dark brew.

"You work outside all day," she countered.

"Here, pretty much. Back in Colorado, I'm all over the place." My cell chimed again.

She glanced at me then back to her dough. "You're a busy lady. I'd think it wouldn't be all that hard to make horse babies."

I arched a brow. "Horse babies?"

She grinned. "I guess horses don't have as much fun as we do practicing, huh?"

I blushed. "You're married to Colton, right? I haven't met him yet."

"Engaged. He and Rob are in Billings looking at metal fencing. Rob's wife, Willow, went with them. Yeah, I'm pretty sure it's as boring as it sounds, and I feel for Willow. But it's guy shopping. Or cowboy shopping. Whatever. Who have you met so far?" she asked, setting dish towels over the loaf pans.

"Clint, obviously. Boyd and Audrey. Johnny. Levi."

She slid the pans across the counter and left them. I assumed they were to rise again although I didn't know much more about bread than it came sliced at the store.

"Levi's cute, don't you think?" she asked as she washed her hands at the sink.

Her back was to me, and I couldn't see her face.

"He's... good-looking." Good-looking enough to

fantasize about him while I used a shower sprayer on my clit.

She spun back around, drying her hands.

"Every guy on Wolf Ranch is hot," she shared. "Sure, I think Colton's extra gorgeous because he's mine and all, but Levi..." She fanned herself.

I wanted to fan myself too because my cheeks were flaming.

She stood on the far side of the counter, leaned down and rested her forearms on the granite. "He's single, you know."

"Levi?"

She tucked her hair behind her ear. "Yes, Levi. He's nice. I give him two thumbs up."

"Does he know you're telling people he's nice?"

She pursed her lips. "Yeah, I doubt any cowboy would want to be called *nice.* He's..." She paused, studied the ceiling as she considered. "Quiet. I'd say a brooder, but all cowboys are content being by themselves. You have to be to live on a ranch in Montana. Winters are brutal. Except maybe Boyd. He's never met a stranger. Levi though, well, I've only been here since last summer, but I'd say he's... misunderstood."

I took the last sip of my coffee. "And you want me to figure him out?" I had no idea where she was going with this, so I stood to help myself to more java.

"I want you to put a smile on his face. However you think is best."

I spun around. Sputtered out a laugh. "Me? What makes you think I can get him to smile?"

She looked me over. "If he doesn't see how pretty and smart you are, then the man needs glasses. And his head checked. I like that belt, by the way."

"Thanks," I said, either for the compliment about my looks or the belt. I liked to always be put together, to look professional, even on a ranch in rural Montana. I put on clean jeans and a red top. I always wore the same gold hoop earrings and never left the house without at least a little makeup.

"You're telling me where you got it later. We girls can do some shopping of our own. Online. We don't even have to drive all the way to Billings."

My cell chimed again. "Sorry, my email sends me notifications."

She stood up and wiped down the counter. "No worries. Get back to your work. We girls get together once a week for ladies happy hour. It's Sunday night. Me, Audrey, Willow, Becky. You'll join us."

Willow. The DEA agent. Was I insane? I didn't have much choice but to say yes. It wasn't like I had other plans. "Um, sure. Thanks."

"Stop up for lunch with the guys later. Dinner's fried chicken. Come with Levi."

When I turned back to look at her from the doorway, she waggled her eyebrows. "Come lots of times with him."

My mouth fell open, then I laughed. What else could I do? Marina was in agreement with my body when it came to Levi. I just had to get my head in gear.

7

HARLIE

"You didn't," my BFF, Keely, shouted into my ear through the phone.

"I did."

"OMG."

"I know. I wanted to die," I admitted, telling her all about how Levi had overheard me getting off in the shower. "I mean, he *knows*." It felt good to have something fun to tell her. I'd been keeping in my problems with Dax because it was too ugly to drag into the light.

I stood up from my bed, unbuttoned my jeans. I was so full from the cinnamon roll, my pants were too tight. If I ate like that every morning I was here, nothing was going to fit.

I'd sent Keely a nine-one-one text first thing this morning, telling her I needed to talk. After tossing and turning all night, I'd texted and said to bring wine and lots of it to our phone call, even at five-thirty in the morning.

Along with Mr. Claymore and one of the trainers, she'd been one of the notification pings on my phone earlier. Said she'd get back to me after she dropped the kids at camp. Which was five minutes ago. Now she wanted to know everything.

"He outright said that he heard?"

"Pretty much but through the door. I didn't have to see his face. Thankfully, he went to his room, and I'd been able to sneak back to mine," I said, dying a little all over again of mortification. "I got dressed to leave, Keel. I had my suitcase on the bed."

"Ah, honey, it's not that bad. I mean, you've got this amazing job. So a guy overheard you flicking the bean. I'm sure he rubs one out a time or two. Everyone does it."

Flicking the bean?

"Yeah, but not when they overhear you calling his name."

She gasped. "You called out his name as you came? He's that gorgeous?"

"He's... hot. Lumberjack. Viking. Caveman. Cowboy. All rolled into one Wrangler-wearing package."

She squealed, and I had to move my phone from my ear.

"I was going to leave. Grab my bags... and Seraphina and leave. Just roll out in the middle of the night and never come back."

"You wouldn't do that."

Sighing, I plopped back down on the bed. "Of course not. I'd lose my job. Pops wouldn't have his medicine. We'd be behind on our bills. Seraphina wouldn't have the perfect little foal next spring. But believe me, I considered all of that, so I didn't have to face Levi."

"Levi. Total cowboy name."

She'd been married to her husband, Brad, for eleven

years. An accountant with a nine-to-five job and a 401k. It seemed she was living vicariously through me, which was ridiculous because I'd done nothing to be jealous of. Not once.

"He heard," I repeated. "Knew I moaned his name. Offered to help."

"He *what?*" she screeched.

"Through the door, he said he would help. I think I'm going to die of shame."

"You will do no such thing, Charlotte Banbrook. If he heard, then he was right at the door. Listening. He's just as pervy as you. He *wants* you."

"He doesn't want me," I protested, even though I knew it wasn't true. I'd seen the way he looked at me, like a starved man at a feast.

"Didn't you say he offered to help? To get you off."

I smoothed out the blanket on the bed, even though it was military precise, even being made at the early hour of five-thirty.

"Yes, but—"

"No buts. Well, his butt. Maybe yours. Maybe he'll spank your butt for being naughty."

I laughed. "He won't spank my butt."

"I bet he will."

A sigh escaped. "He won't. He might be interested, but he doesn't know."

"Of course, he doesn't. It's not like you have a big scarlet V on your shirt. You're a virgin, hon, not a freak."

"I'm a thirty-year-old virgin. A guy like Levi would run away screaming if he knew."

"So you've been burned in the past. That doesn't mean this guy's an asshole like other guys you went out with."

I grabbed the pillow, hugged it to my chest.

"How long are you there?" she wondered.

"Two to three weeks. Depending on Seraphina."

"Fine. While she's getting it on with a stallion who's probably hung like a horse." She laughed at her own horrible joke. I stayed silent. "You should get it on with a stallion of your own. I wonder if he's hung like a horse, too."

"Keely!" I cried, rolling my eyes. "I have no idea how big his dick is." I flushed hotly and dropped my voice. "He does have huge hands though."

She laughed. "Go for it. Have a fling. Get that V-card punched with a sexy cowboy."

I didn't tell her he's also the sheriff. It didn't make any difference to her. Hot sheriff, hot cowboy...

"I'm here to work."

"Not all the time, and besides, you work way too much. I'm sure no one there expects you to punch a clock or work on those crazy spreadsheets of yours all the time."

"I'm sure they don't expect me to screw one of the ranch hands, either." I thought of Marina and what she'd said. Maybe there was one person here who thought it was a good idea.

"People have sex, honey. All the time. Get in on the fun."

"I don't do casual," I reminded her. "I'm looking for a serious relationship."

"I know you don't do casual. You don't do anyone. Levi can be a fling. A short term thing. You know going in that it's got an expiration date. That's good."

I didn't say anything.

"I'm not saying marry the guy," she continued. "Have sex. Lots of sex in all kinds of positions. Use him. I'm sure he won't mind." She groaned. "Please, Charlie. Have. Some. Fun."

She punctuated every word because I was a workaholic.

"Fine. I'll think about it." Maybe sex was what I needed. To clear my head, help me relax, so I could figure my way out of my situation.

"Say it. Say you'll do it."

I hopped to my feet, tossed the pillow aside, paced.

"Repeat after me. I, Charlie Banbrook, oldest living virgin."

"Shut up." I laughed.

"Say it or I'll tell your grandfather you were the one who broke his favorite coffee mug."

I narrowed my eyes, but she couldn't see me. "That's low, girlfriend." Pops had loved that mug, and we'd tried to glue it back together to no success when it had broken when we were sixteen.

"Say it."

Sighing, I muttered her words aloud. "I, Charlie Banbrook, oldest living virgin."

"Good job," she praised. "Will screw the hot cowboy living down the hall."

I glanced at my closed bedroom door, wondering if he was standing outside again. I tiptoed to it, opened it and peeked out. The hall was deserted. Sighing, I shut the door and repeated Keely's words. "I will screw the hot cowboy living down the hall."

"More than once."

"More than once."

"I will have fun doing it."

"Are you done yet?" I questioned.

"Say it."

"I will have fun doing it."

"And I will tell my best friend every naughty detail."

I laughed at that, dropped back onto the bed.

"Fine. I'll do it. But how?"

"Ah, honey. All you have to do is go up to him, give him a smile and say *yes*."

Yes. Was it really that simple?

Maybe I would give the cowboy a ride.

8

 EVI

CHARLIE WAS A VIRGIN.

Mind blown. Dick hard.

I'd overheard her phone conversation with her friend this morning when she came in after mating the horses. At least her half of the call. I had great shifter hearing and couldn't help but eavesdrop, especially after she said *he's... hot*. Then when she'd continued to talk, and I'd learned so much more about her. Not just the fact that no guy had taken her before. That she didn't see sex as something fun, something hot. Sweaty. Pleasurable. Memorable. Mind erasing. She saw it as a... a hurdle. Something that was unsurmountable. An actual problem.

I had to wonder if it was because someone had treated her wrong, but the more she'd talked, the more it just seemed she'd just never been seduced, never *wanted* to be seduced before.

Now she felt as if there was something wrong with her, and that was just fucking sad. I would never want a woman to think she wasn't desirable. Passionate. Confident.

Based on what I'd heard in the shower the night before, she could get off and wasn't shy about pleasuring herself. That was a good start. I was making it my job to get her the rest of the way.

Well and truly fucked. Mussed. Sweaty. Dripping with her need. Filthy with my cum. Screaming with pleasure. Again and again.

At dawn, I heard her get up and leave the bunkhouse to meet up with Clint. Today was the first day of hand breeding, and I knew the two of them would start early. I hadn't dared join them, horned up as I was, and instead took a truck and went up into the hills to repair one of the washed out backroads.

She was here for work, and I wouldn't shame or fluster her, even unintentionally, while she was doing her job. Of course, I wouldn't shame her when she wasn't either. Knowing now about her and sex, I'd made the right choice. Her work was work. What I shared with her would be separate from that. I would respect her in all ways, especially in this.

She was well educated, had a good job, was trusted in it. I wouldn't fuck with that no matter how much I wanted her.

Besides all that, I had to get myself in check. I'd barely slept all night, tossing and fucking turning. Restless and frustrated. If I'd been able to shift, I'd have run and burned off the excess energy. Instead, I'd fought with myself not to smash down Charlie's door and show her what should happen when she screamed my name. I'd hopped in the shower and rubbed one out, my cum arcing from my dick in thick ropes. It had eased my need. Briefly... because my cock stayed hard.

Knowing Charlie was just down the hall... She was all I thought about. Gorgeous. Funny. Smart. Perfect. A virgin.

How was that even possible? A woman that beautiful? But she *was* reserved. Some might even call her uptight. She wasn't shy. No. She was warm and friendly when you cornered her. But she was... *busy.* She seemed to never stop working. Or thinking. She was probably the type who had trouble letting go. Definitely after what I'd heard of her phone call. Getting vulnerable and intimate wasn't her thing.

Pot, meet kettle. Or kettle, meet pot—whatever the damned saying was.

I'd been horny before. I'd had the need to get laid like any guy. I just had never been obsessed with a woman until Doctor Delicious climbed out of that truck yesterday and blew my entire life to pieces.

She was attracted to me. No doubt about that. Not after I heard her come as she called out my name. Not after what she'd told her friend. I heard every fucking word. And she wanted me to punch that V-card for her.

Oh, I'd punch it. I'd punch it hard. I'd punch it so well and so long she'd never look anywhere else for a man or for sex.

I had two weeks. Two weeks until she took her pretty ass and fancy horse back to Colorado. As she'd told her friend, she'd have sex with me... and have fun doing it. I'd make sure of it. Abso-fucking-lutely.

With that goal in mind, I sauntered down the central corridor of the stable. She was in the stall with Seraphina. I heard her, the clicking of her fingers on a keyboard. She was a fucking workaholic. She was the first person to ever work on a computer in a horse stall around here. I leaned against the half door and knocked. Silly, yes, but I didn't want to scare her.

She sat on a stool she must have found... somewhere. Her head whipped around, and her eyes widened. Her cell dropped to the hay-covered ground. "Levi."

My name on her lips, all breathy and full of surprise, made me fucking hard. *Harder.*

"Hey, doll." I opened the half door and stepped in. Slowly. I had two fillies I didn't want to startle. I hadn't seen her since the night before.

She stood, setting her laptop on the stool she'd just vacated. I stepped closer. She didn't move back.

"Working?" I asked.

She nodded. "Catching up on emails, adding data to Seraphina's charts."

Here I'd thought being a vet for Mr. Claymore was a cush job, getting a mare to a breeder and ensuring it took. Apparently Charlie didn't see it that way.

I looked to the beautiful horse who was eyeing me, her ears flicked back. "Everything going okay?"

I hadn't heard otherwise from Clint, so I was just making small talk.

"So far, so good. She'll be bred again the day after tomorrow. Did you need something?" she asked.

I gave her a small smile. "Actually, I'm here to offer *you* something." I tipped my hat. "My services."

Seraphina nickered, as if she found me amusing.

"Excuse me?" The crisp white blouse from the day before was replaced with a plaid button-up. Little pearl snaps drew my eye to the swell of her breasts. She wore a pretty plum shade of lipstick on her pillowy lips and mascara today.

That was new. Was it for me? I sure as fuck hoped it was. It was totally unnecessary, of course, but I wouldn't mind it if she was thinking about me when she dressed this morning. I had to wonder if she'd taken this much care on the outside, what was she wearing beneath? Lavender lace would look gorgeous on her.

"Cowboy services," I said. "I may or may not have overheard you were in need of them. Please tell me I was the cowboy down the hall you were contemplating screwing. Because if it was Johnny, I'll have to throat-punch him."

Her eyes widened the moment she caught on to what I was talking about. She flushed, but a choked laugh came out of her. "Oh God. You heard that, too? I'm seriously going to die."

"Nah, nothing shameful about knowing what you want. I like when a woman is aware of what she needs."

Her gaze darted around, as if she could see outside the stall. "At least Johnny didn't hear. Where is he anyway? I haven't seen him since I moved in."

"I kicked him out of the bunkhouse," I admitted, without a bit of remorse. "I'm the one in danger of dying, doll. I keep thinking about you in the shower last night. Now I find out you're in need of my services."

"Services?" The word came out just over a whisper.

I arched a brow. She glanced away.

"I'm here with an offer."

The thrum of her pulse made my wolf want to howl. The way her chest heaved, I'd made her breathless. Eager. Nervous. Still, she covered it well, cocking a hip and raising her brows. "Wh-what offer?"

I wasn't going to skirt around the topic. We only had so

much time. Not only because she was going back to Colorado but because I was going to lose my shit if I didn't have her. "Two weeks. That's how long you're here, right?"

She looked suspicious, cocking her head to the side, but nodded.

"Give me those fourteen nights to pleasure you."

It was perfect. I had no intention of marrying a human, but this arrangement had a built in deadline. It could be short-term and casual without anyone's heart getting broken. I'd take care of her needs, just as she'd told the person on the phone she wanted. And she'd slake this lust she'd produced in me. I'd get her out of my system before I found my true mate. *If* I found her. Until then, why not a little fun?

Her mouth opened and closed in surprise. "Wh-what do you mean?"

A smile tugged at my lips. "Oh, I think it's pretty obvious, isn't it? You need your V-card punched with a—" I cleared my throat. "—hot cowboy."

I was dying to touch her, but I waited, still not sure if she would pull back. "I'll punch that card for you, and I promise I'll make it good. I'll keep punching it every night you're here. You know—to make up for lost time." My mouth stretched into a fierce grin. I reached for her waist and lightly settled my hand there to see if she'd accept my touch.

She did. Her gaze locked mine, the warm brown of her irises darkened with blown pupils. For a moment she didn't breathe.

Neither did I.

"You want to... to have sex with me."

"Yes."

"For two weeks."

"Yes."

She was getting it. "A fling."

"A fling," I repeated.

She blinked, glanced between my eyes to assess my... sincerity? "Okay."

I let out my breath. *Okay?*

She sounded unsure. Almost startled by her answer as if the words fell out of her mouth without thinking.

"Okay. Starting now." I didn't give her time to second-guess. I immediately tugged her close and slammed my lips down on hers. I backed her into one of the stall walls, ensuring we were away from Seraphina, especially her back half. The kiss might make me feel like I'd been kicked in the gut, but I didn't really want it to happen.

Charlie gasped against my mouth, stumbling a little before I wrapped my arm tightly behind her back and pulled her lithe body up against mine even closer.

"N-now?" she squeaked when I broke the kiss. "Here?"

"Here. Now. Or anytime. Make that *every* time. Every time you get horny, Charlie, you skip that showerhead and come to me. Your pussy aches, I'll fill it. Your clit's hard, I'll lick and suck it. I'll take care of all your needs. That's a promise." I cupped her ass with one hand, squeezing and kneading. Fuck, she was soft and round, perfect in my palm.

"Um." She was nervous. She didn't know what to do. How could she? My oh-so-serious veterinarian had never been with anyone. Until me. And, I was guessing, was the kind of woman who was always up in her head. Had trouble letting her hair down.

"Shh." I spun her around, so she didn't have to worry about hiding her expression from me. I molded my hand over her mons, rubbing slowly between her legs over the seam of her jeans. "Your job is just to receive. Receive and tell me what you like. What you want more of. What feels good." I nipped at her ear. "Can you do that for me?"

She mewled at the added pressure I put on her clit.

"Gotta hear the words, doll."

"I... I—" Her eyes fell closed, and she sighed, as if letting go. Giving over. "Yes," she breathed.

I unbuttoned the jeans and slid my hand inside her panties. She jerked when my fingertip brushed over her bare sex. I stroked lightly over her clit, then lower to gather her nectar. I watched her breath catch, the way her pulse thrummed at her neck.

"You want this?"

"Yes... okay." She still sounded breathless but verified she was good to go. There was no question she was hot for it.

I was going to keep her that way.

I kissed her neck. "Did I make you ache down here?" I rubbed a slow circle around the swollen bud of her clit.

"Ehm... wow." Her head fell against my shoulder, as if I was slowly loosening her muscles. Melting her bones. I took it as another win. Every time she let go a little more, I would count it as success. I moved my fingers lower again and slowly screwed one into her. Carefully.

"Oh... ah." Her fingers snagged my forearm, and she held on.

She was tight. So damn tight. I'd have to make sure I really prepared her before I sank my dick between her legs because the thought of causing her any pain destroyed me. I'd have to build up to sex slowly. There was so much to show her, so many ways to get her to come before I even did. I pumped my finger a few times, then eased it out to make another trip around her clit.

"Does that feel good, Doc?" I breathed against her neck, licked her delicate skin.

"Yes." Her immediate response sent satisfaction humming through me. I couldn't wait for her to call my name like she had in the shower the night before. I pushed my finger inside her again, grinding the heel of my hand against her clit as I did. She brought her fingers down on top of mine, pushing me deeper.

"You want more?" Just the knowledge that no other guy had done this, that I was the first to witness her pleasure made my dick hard. Maybe it was a caveman thing, but I wanted to howl that I was claiming something so sweet.

"Yes," she gasped.

I worked a second finger inside her, and she sobbed out a breath.

"Oh God."

"Do me a favor, Doc," I murmured in her ear, still working my fingers inside her and my palm against her clit. "Moan my name again when you come, like you did last night."

She shook her head, but her breath was ragged, her pelvis undulated against my hand.

"Say it," I encouraged.

"No," she whimpered.

"Which cowboy are you going to ride while you're here?"

She choked, her belly shuddering against my forearm, then gasped, "Levi!" Her muscles squeezed around my fingers as she came, her walls pulsing with her release.

"That's right, doll," I said, watching her come. Her eyes were closed, her mouth open, her breathing ragged. That mind of hers wasn't thinking about anything at all but the pleasure I gave her. Fuck, yes. "I'm the guy who's going to make you come. Every. Damn. Time."

 HARLIE

OH WOW. Sex with a partner was way better than on my own. Exponentially better. So good I started giggling because the whole thing was so ridiculous. Seraphina nickered and shifted in the stall.

I wasn't the type to let a man get his hands down my pants in a stable.

Especially not a cowboy. And yet, Levi had his hand down my pants. In a stable. With Seraphina watching.

"This is crazy," I laughed as he slipped his hand free then slid his fingers in his mouth.

Oh my.

He kept his eyes on me as he did it, and I listened to the growl that ripped from his chest. It was one of the most carnal things I'd ever seen. My pussy clenched on nothing. The feel of his fingers lingered.

He was so skilled, and that was all he'd used. His fingers.

What could he do if he got his entire body into it? And we weren't in the stable when he did so.

He helped me zip my jeans.

"What about you?" I wondered. He hadn't gotten off, and I could see the thick bulge of his dick pressing against his pants. That couldn't be comfortable.

His hands stayed at my waist, but his gaze lifted to mine. "I'm not taking you for the first time in the stable. I want a bed and hours where we can figure out what makes you hot, what gets you off."

"Oh," I breathed.

Seraphina snuffled and brought me out of my orgasm-induced fog.

"I can't believe we just did that in here." I looked up at him through my lashes.

"No?"

I shook my head. "I, uh, had a strict no-fling rule. Especially people I work with."

His forehead wrinkled. "That right?" He looked more bothered by it than he should.

To ease the sting, I shared. "It's hard to be a woman in a man's world. I have to ensure I'm seen as qualified for my job because of my experience and skills, and I don't mean between the sheets. I really shouldn't be with you here because you're the client, but... "

He smiled. "I'd say that since Eddison's fucking your mare, there's probably a gray area."

I pursed my lips, so I didn't laugh. He had a point. I wasn't going after Clint who was the Wolf Ranch representative I was working with, and it was Eddison who had to prove himself more than me.

Levi's expression softened. "I'm sorry you have to validate your abilities because you're a woman. It's hard enough in any job proving you're worthy. Like me, the cowboy sheriff." He grinned.

A prickle of warning ran through me at the word *sheriff,* but my body felt so good from the orgasm, I shoved it away.

My cell rang, and I startled. Levi stepped back, and I grabbed my cell from my back pocket. "Oh! It's my grandfather. Hang on, I have to take this." I held up a finger, wincing.

"Of course." He nodded and angled his body away, as if to give me privacy. He turned to Seraphina and rubbed her nose.

"Hi, Pops," I said, a pang of guilt running through me at leaving him for these two weeks. My gram had died two years ago, and he'd been getting increasingly confused. Forgetful. While I'd lived close by before, I'd moved back in with him this past year to make sure he was okay.

That situation hadn't helped my love life, either. Yet with my parents retired and happily playing shuffleboard in Florida, Pops was my only family around.

"Charlie?" My grandfather croaked into the phone.

"Hi, yes, it's me."

He cleared his throat. "Well... where are you? I've been waiting on you for the ice cream."

I swallowed back my anguish over his deteriorating mental state. "I'm in Montana, remember? For work. I'm breeding Seraphina. Remember that pretty horse I took you to see last week?"

"That's right. How are things going up there?"

I glanced to Levi. "Good. Things are going good. Did Mrs. Vasquez stop by for dinner?"

"She did. Meatloaf. Mashed potatoes *and* gravy. I know how much you dislike gravy."

His forgetfulness was a tricky thing. Inconsistent. "That's right. I hate gravy."

"Well, I'm sure you're busy with your work. I've got a good book, and I want to know how it ends."

He sounded better now, just that quick moment of confusion over ice cream. "All right, I'll call you tomorrow. Love you, Pops."

"Right back at you, sweetpea."

I hung up and tucked the phone back in my pocket.

"She all set for the night?" Levi asked, tipping his head toward Seraphina, patting her flank then facing me.

I nodded and collected my things. Levi grabbed the stool, and we cleared out of her stall. He led me to the main doors, and he left the stool there then closed them behind us.

"You're close with your grandfather, I take it."

We walked side by side to the bunkhouse. It wasn't dark yet, but the sun had slipped behind the mountains. Crickets chirped, and the wind blew through the grass. It was lovely. Peaceful. Or it may have been me relaxed from a man-induced orgasm.

Having Levi beside me... the guy who'd had his hands on me... in me? I liked being with him. Beside him. I liked *him*.

Keely was right. I should have fun. I should have Levi. Why not?

He looked at me, and I realized he was waiting for an answer to his question.

"Oh um, yes. I live with him now. I noticed he was forgetting stuff since my grandma died. Little things. He'd ask me the same question five minutes apart. He's eighty, and I worried about him being alone all the time."

"He's all right with you away?"

"The neighbor is keeping an eye on him. It's getting worse, I won't deny it. Soon I'll have to make decisions about his care." Tears threatened, and I blinked them away. "Sorry, grandparents are special, you know?"

He stopped just outside the bunkhouse door. He sighed, took off his hat and looked down at the ground. "I moved in with my grandparents when I was fourteen after my parents died. They hated my dad for taking my mom away from them." His voice was flat, and it was clear this was a sore subject for him.

I set my hand on his arm.

He offered me a quick glance. "It's not bad like it sounds. My parents loved each other. Desperately. But that didn't matter to my grandparents. They blamed my father for her death. And I looked like him."

"They took their grief out on you," I said, my voice soft.

He stared out at the prairie, seeing the past, not the tall grass. "My grandparents weren't kind people. I'll just leave it at that. I left the minute I turned eighteen. Never went back."

I could tell there was much he wasn't saying. Four years of hurt and... worse.

"What's this about gravy?" he asked, clearly switching topics. I went with it.

"Pops likes gravy. I detest anything drowning my food."

"I like gravy," he said, his smile returning. He opened the door for me.

"I'm sure you do. A big cowboy like you is always hungry."

He hooked my hip and pulled me into him. I had to tilt my head back to meet his eyes.

"I'm hungry now," he said, his voice going deep. "I had a taste of you on my fingers, and I want more."

"Oh," I said.

He took my bag from me, carefully set it beside the door.

"I want to get you naked. Get you in my bed. Get between those thighs and eat you out. You'll come, doll. Again and again until I get my fill. Okay with you?"

He waited. I processed and let my body melt under the heat of his stare. Turn soft and pliant like pulled taffy.

Was that okay with me? Hell yes, it was.

"Race you to the stairs." I took off at a sprint. I heard his heavy footfalls behind me, and I squealed with laughter. Yeah, maybe I could have some fun with a sexy cowboy. Especially if he wanted to eat me out.

EVI

WHY THE FUCK had I been so butthurt about having a human under my roof? Now I was in seventh heaven.

Charlie couldn't know it, but chase was a game all wolves loved. Even for me, a shifter who'd never shifted. She bolted across the main room, and my wolf howled. I grinned and took off after her, easily catching up and tossing her into my arms with my superior strength.

She shrieked and giggled, then covered her mouth, as if giggling was something she never did.

"I'm gonna keep you screaming all night," I warned, but I kept my tone playful, so I wouldn't make her nervous. It was her first time, and she was human. I'd have to dial back my usual sexual aggression. Not too much because I wasn't going to hide who I was from her, but I'd save the hard fucking for round two.

I was like a sex-starved teenager again around her. My dick was always hard. I was hyper-focused on having sex. I thought about it day and night. I jerked off like I was sixteen, more than once a day. And damn, my teenage years had been rough—sexual repression mixed with wolf repression had made for an extremely grumpy and maladjusted young man.

Now? I still had to hide that I was a wolf, but Charlie was game to get down. She wasn't a virgin on prom night. We weren't going to fumble around in the backseat of a car.

I'd get her bare, get her beneath me and get in her. I'd make it good for her, too. If the way she got off on my hand was any indication, she'd take to my dick easily enough.

I carried Charlie to my bedroom, only because my bed was bigger, and I wanted room to really spread her thighs and show her heaven. I kicked open my door and tossed her down on my king.

"You remember your job?" I asked as I tossed my cowboy hat on the dresser and stripped off my shirt.

It was a mistake. I shouldn't have taken my hands off Charlie because she looked like she was in her head again, coming up to sit awkwardly on the mattress and staring at me.

I tackled her to her back, pinning her wrists beside her head. "Hmm?" I was holding her down, but if she showed any indication of nerves or changing her mind, I'd let her up. I'd watched her mind go blank earlier, and I'd do it again.

If there was someone who needed to come hard and often, it was the little vet pressed beneath me.

"Um." She rubbed her full lips together.

"Your job is to tell me what you like and don't like," I reminded her.

She relaxed, and that release, that giving over, fucking did something to me. "Got it."

I worked the pearl snaps on her shirt. "That's your only job. You let me worry about the rest. Okay?"

Relief swam in her warm brown eyes. She nodded her agreement and let me slip the blouse down her shoulders and off her arms. "Mmm. This is pretty." She wore a pale pink bra, which set off her dark skin. Fucking beautiful.

"Matching set?" I asked, flicking open the button on her jeans and sliding them down her legs. She shifted her hips to help me, toeing off one boot then the other, letting them thump to the floor.

Dayum. It *was* a matching set. The satin and lace panties made her look like a goddess stretched out on my bed. Her skin all but glowed in the evening light coming through the window.

"You are so beautiful." I straddled her and dropped a kiss between her breasts, then above her belly button. Below it. I kissed the fabric of her panties, right above her clit. I nipped her labia through the silky material then her inner thigh.

I rolled her to her belly and gently bit her ass, making her gasp, the look over her shoulder at me. I grinned wolfishly. Yeah, I was going to show her *everything.*

Her body was lean, but her ass was full and round, the perfect combination of muscle beneath a soft cushion. I gave it a gentle slap, remembering how she'd mentioned being spanked in her phone call.

She bit her lip, and that little crease in her forehead showed those wheels in her head were turning again.

"Did you like that?"

Her breath came in short pants. "I-I think so."

I slapped the other cheek. "You tell me more when you

want more, or go on when you want me to try something else."

"More," she murmured, barely over a whisper.

She bit her lip, clearly worried that one word had come out. That she'd told me what she liked, that she'd wanted something a little naughty. But a playful spanking wasn't the dirtiest thing we'd do. She just didn't know it yet.

"That's my girl." I gave her another slap, a little harder. She didn't flinch, only gave a little whimper, then a delicious hip roll. I spanked her ass a few more times, then hoisted her hips up until her knees came under her. When I unhooked her bra, it fell open to the sides. Reaching underneath her chest, I pinched her nipple into a stiff, hard peak. I stroked her ass, squeezing and kneading it, then gripping her hips. It was a position I wanted to fuck her in.

Desperately.

I wouldn't—not tonight, anyway—but the sight of her ass in the air, waiting for me, got me hotter than hell.

I rubbed my fingers between her legs over her panties. They were damp with her arousal, and I pushed them to the side and stroked over her wet folds.

She startled, then stilled when I began to play. So wet. So hot. So plush and swollen.

I had to taste her.

Now.

I pulled her panties down, and she straightened her legs and dropped back to her belly to let me take them off her, shaking off her bra at the same time. She was right there with me. Naked.

"Screaming is allowed," I said as I pushed her to her side and hooked my hand under the top knee to pull it up and open. "So is hair tugging. Any guy been here before?"

She frowned, then shook her head.

"Okay, doll. You said you were a virgin, but I wasn't sure how much you played. I have to admit, knowing I'm the first guy to get here, to get my mouth on you..." I reached down and pressed hard against my dick to get control again.

I ignored her uncertain look as I lowered my head and licked into her.

She gasped, jerking hard.

I tsked. "Hold still for me, doll. I need to taste you."

I flicked the tip of my tongue against the hood of her clit lightly several times, then swirled my tongue around it with more pressure.

Her moan was a sweet reward. I traced the inside of her sex, sucked and nipped her labia.

Her legs thrashed around my shoulders, and she reached for my hair, tugging tentatively at first, then with more force. It only made me impossibly harder.

"That's right, doll. Show me where you want my mouth." I made my tongue stiff and penetrated her, but she tugged my face higher. I got my lips over her little nubbin and sucked and she cried out, yanking my hair.

I worked one finger inside her and pumped it as her legs went wild around me. Then I worked a second in and curled them to stroke her inner wall, seeking that elusive G-spot. She started vocalizing—letting out short gasps and choked cries. Little keening syllables of need.

"Yes... ung... please... oh!"

I found the place where the tissue felt different— stiffened and raised under my fingertips and worked the spot, listening to her cries grow more frantic. My dick surged against my zipper, rock hard and aching, but tonight wasn't about me. I needed to get my sexy veterinarian comfortable with letting go and allowing herself to experience pleasure with a male—*me*—before I even thought about popping her cherry.

She'd already come once in the stable, and she was almost there for number two. I'd get more off her until she knew she was a wild, passionate woman. Until her brain was empty, and all she could think about was how I made her feel.

By the time our two weeks were through, Charlie would never have trouble asking for—even demanding—what she wanted or needed from a man.

Except thinking of Charlie with another male stirred some deep-seated jealousy I'd never experienced before, which had me working her pussy with even more intent. Her orgasms were mine. It wasn't like me to be possessive of the human females I fucked. Not by a long shot. Strange that this one evoked something primitive in me. Primitive? Hell, yes. She was so beautiful like this, lost, wild in her complete abandon. And I was doing it to her.

I was fierce in my determination to show her everything.

But I forgot all that the moment Charlie cried out and came all over my face. I pumped my fingers in and out of her as her tight channel squeezed and fluttered, pelvic floor lifting and pulling up. She dripped onto me, my palm drenched, my lips and chin covered.

"Oh my God. Oh my *gawd*!" she moaned. "Levi."

"That's right, doll," I said, licking my lips. "I love it when you say my name while you come."

"Oh God."

"Levi will do," I deadpanned, pulling my fingers out of her and licking them, too.

She pushed up on her elbows, her dark hair mussed, face flushed. "Wow."

I grinned, feeling more than a little pleased with myself. "I haven't even punched that V-card for you, yet."

Her flush grew brighter, and she flopped on her back and stared at the ceiling. "Wow," she repeated.

"I'll get you some water. We need to keep you hydrated." I winked before I slipped out of the room to grab a cold bottle of water from the fridge. When I came back, I was half afraid she'd be getting dressed or hiding under the covers, but she hadn't moved. She still lay gloriously naked in the center of my bed, her muscles slack, a small smile on her face.

I'd put it there.

I fucking loved knowing that.

 HARLIE

Wow. I couldn't stop saying it.

Or thinking it.

I'd never orgasmed so hard in my life. Battery operated boyfriends and showerheads did not compare to a real partner. And he'd done it not once, but twice.

His attention to detail was... impressive. And he was still clothed.

Levi cracked open a bottle of cold water and handed it to me. I stared at him as I sipped. I really wasn't sure how it happened that I suddenly had this hot cowboy's undivided attention on me and my body. On my lady parts. I'd never attracted that much male attention before. Probably because I didn't put out the vibe. That's what Keely always told me, anyway.

He'd made it so I had zero doubt he was into me. As I

said, he was still wearing his clothes! Any guy only interested in getting off would have been naked, in me, finished and out the door by now. But Levi? I'd come twice... and I hadn't even seen his dick.

That dick, though, looked like the size of a large cucumber in his pants, but he still didn't seem to be in a hurry to get his own needs met. I swallowed, looking at the bulge. Because soon—very soon—that big cock was going to be between my legs.

"Why am I the only one naked here?" I blurted, starting to get nervous about the whole thing.

He grinned and in one smooth motion, pulled his t-shirt over his head with one hand. "You wanna see the goods?"

My face grew warm. Did I? Um, hell yes, I did! Judging from his massive, muscled bare torso, the rest of him was going to be magnificent. "Yep. Show me what you've got, Sheriff."

My smile slipped when I realized what I said, but I couldn't go there now. This wasn't the time to get back in my head and panic. Or freak. Or... think. Keely said to have fun, and I was going to have fun, even if it killed me. Death by orgasm.

His smile grew wider as he stripped out of his jeans and boxers and crawled onto the bed.

I drew a sharp breath.

Hung like a horse did actually sum it up.

Oh shit.

That thing was supposed to fit inside me. I stared at it. Long and thick with a flared crown. The color of it was darker than the rest of him. A pearly bead of pre-cum appeared at the slit.

My inner walls clenched.

He chuckled as he climbed over me. "It'll fit." Damned mind reader.

"I know," I said, sounding more defensive than I meant to. My brain was already running through everything I knew about breeding horses. And humans. I was properly aroused. I would stretch to accommodate him.

Wouldn't I?

"We don't have to do this tonight," he said, probably reading my anxiety.

"No!" I said quickly. I was not going to get this close to losing my virginity and chicken out. That would just be stupid. "We're doing this. I'm not a prom date to deflower. It's not that big of a deal."

He was huge and every part of him was hard as brick, but he let me push him onto his back, so I was above him. He stretched one long arm toward the nightstand where a box of condoms was tucked away and pulled one out as I straddled him.

Save a horse, ride a cowboy, as they said.

I could do this. I could definitely do this.

Levi's eyes were heavy-lidded as he rolled the condom over his member. God, he should be proud of that thing.

"I like it when you take charge, Doc. Work yourself down onto me. You just use me as your own personal fuck-toy. Get yourself off and don't worry about me. You can't do anything wrong, and I'm gonna enjoy every fucking second of it." His hands settled at my hips, and he gave me a little squeeze.

I loved his reassurances. I wasn't sure how he even knew to give them. I doubted he was the type who took a woman's virginity often, especially considering his age and attractiveness. Hell, unless he went after teenagers, there weren't many like me left at our age. I was probably the only thirty-year old virgin in Montana. Not for long.

Maybe my nerves were that transparent. I took a deep breath, looked down at Levi. He was relaxed, but aroused. Patient, but eager. Needy, but patient. Everything about him had me relaxing. I was wet. Primed. Two orgasms had me relaxed-ish. I could do this.

Everything receded but the feel of Levi beneath me. The soft prickles of the hairs on his legs against mine. The feel of his breathing beneath my palms on his chest.

His reassuring gaze. No, it was the heat I saw, the need... for me that had me nodding. I'd made him this way. Hard and ready to fuck.

Levi gripped the base of his cock and held it steady for me, and I lifted my hips and lowered myself onto him slowly. The broad head settled at my entrance, and because I was so wet, it pushed inside. Gravity helped, and he stretched me open. I gasped at the feel.

A shiver of pleasure ran through me. It felt good.

So good.

Levi groaned, his nostrils flaring. He looked down at the place where my flesh parted to accept his, eyes almost seeming to glow in the lamplight.

"That's so hot, Charlie."

Something about hearing him say my name in that rough, hungry voice made my pussy squeeze around the tip of his cock. I lowered some more.

He thrust up in response, and I gasped at the sudden stretch. "Sorry! Sorry, doll. It just felt so good. You keep squeezing my dick like that, and you're going to find yourself on your back getting nailed like a porn star."

I choked out a laugh, but his teasing relaxed me, and I

took him a little deeper, and then deeper until I sat fully on his lap.

He closed his eyes and gripped my hips, fingers pressing into my flesh as if he was trying to rein in his desire.

"You okay? That didn't hurt at all?" he wondered.

"A virgin only means never having a dick in you before. I've played with more than the showerhead. Besides, horseback riding takes care of those kinds of things, too."

I had no idea how my hymen had broken. I didn't care. There was no pain with him being in me, but it was uncomfortable trying to accommodate him.

I rocked once, slowly, testing the movement.

Oh God. Yeah, that wasn't uncomfortable at all.

It felt incredible. I rocked forward, rubbing my clit down against his body as I took him deeper inside me. And then I couldn't get enough of that motion. I braced my hands on his shoulders and quickened my pace, riding him fast in a forward and back trajectory, getting the full benefit of the friction against my clit.

"That's it, doll."

The room filled with frantic sounds, which I realized were coming from me. Levi's eyes glowed brighter, his fingers gripped tighter. He helped me, taking over the work by pulling and pushing my hips and then somehow knowing it was time for a change. He lifted and lowered my hips over his cock, bouncing me in the air.

He did fit. Every inch.

I dropped my head back, losing all self-consciousness in the sheer pleasure of it. Finding abandon, perhaps for the first time in my life. "Levi," I gasped.

He growled and bounced me faster. "Fuck, yeah, Charlie."

"Oh my God... I can't... I'm going to... oh Levi!" I exploded into pleasure as my orgasm came on so hard I lost my bearings. The room spun. I couldn't focus. It didn't matter because Levi had stopped thrusting up into me and held my hips tight to his, his manhood spearing me so deep I felt him against my cervix. My hips bucked a few times and shudders ran through me as wave after wave of intense release ran through me.

When my vision returned, I found myself staring at the ceiling. I'd thrown my head back, tits to the sky, like a goddess calling in her power through the act of sex.

I found Levi's face. He hadn't gone to outer space like me. His focus was glued intently to my face, and he watched me, as if fascinated. "Did you—"

He scoff-laughed. "Oh yeah. Trust me, doll. That blew my mind."

Was that possible? Could a virgin blow a hot cowboy-sheriff's mind? Or was he just trying to make me feel good?

I didn't take him for a smooth talker. He was easy to talk to but didn't strike me as someone who didn't speak the truth. It wasn't like he could fake it.

Levi eased his firm grip on my hips and stroked his palms around my ass and down my thighs. "You feel good, doll? Sore?"

I shook my head. "No." I offered a smile. "You *are* big, but no. You must've done a good job preparing me."

He pulled me down on top of him and kissed me hard. Possessively. His hand snaked around behind my head and held me captive as his tongue swept between my lips. Our bodies were still connected, and he thrust up into me, mimicking the movement of his tongue.

I moaned into his mouth, my sex still tingling and swollen with arousal, my libido fully unlocked.

"You're incredible," he murmured when he broke the kiss. "Stay in my bed tonight?"

"Oh! Um..." I hadn't been prepared for that offer. This was just two weeks of hot sex.

That had been the deal, right? I'd assumed sex meant sex not sleeping.

"I don't know," I said lamely, extricating our bodies and rolling off to the side. I hissed when he slipped out. Okay, yeah, I was a little sore. "I need to be up early to run tests on Seraphina."

He rolled the other way, getting up to dispose of the condom. "Right, of course."

Did he sound stiff? Or was I reading too much into this?

I hopped off the bed and looked around for my panties. They were on the floor with the rest of our clothes. I slid my feet into them and pulled them up, then grabbed Levi's T-shirt.

I brought it to my face and inhaled. It smelled delicious —like leather and man. I tugged it over my head. I didn't know why—maybe I really didn't want to leave. I wanted some piece of him to take back to my room with me.

When he turned around and saw me in it, his blank expression softened. "I like you in my shirt. Definitely looks better on you." His appreciative gaze landed on my chest where my nipples tented the fabric.

"Is it okay if I wear it back to my room?"

He spread his big hands. "Be my guest, doll. I like knowing I'll be sleeping with you in some form." He seemed totally comfortable in his full nudity—no less powerful or commanding that he'd been in his ranch clothes.

Huh. I blinked at him.

He sure seemed attached for a guy who had outlined the rules to a purely sexual relationship.

But what did I know? I'd never even had a sexual relationship before. I was leaving as soon as the breeding was complete. I'd be back in Colorado soon, far from here. Far from Levi. This was a fling. I'd keep it at that, so I grabbed my clothes and shoes from his floor. "Thanks, um, yeah. Thanks. For everything."

"You come back if you need more," he said lightly, but I could've sworn I saw a frown between his brows. His dick wasn't as hard as before, but it sure wasn't hanging flaccid between his legs. It was as if he were primed for another go.

"Tomorrow night," I promised. I'd protect my heart, but that didn't mean I didn't want more. Lots more. It was as if the seal had been broken, and I wanted all I could get. "Right? Fourteen nights?"

"Damn straight. As for tomorrow, I have a shift as sheriff. I'll be busy because the county fair's going on."

"That sounds fun."

He tilted his head. "You want to go? I'll take you after I get off."

Now that sounded like a date because I doubted he meant we were going to have sex there. I was getting more confused by the minute. And yet I found myself incapable of refusing. I could think of nothing more enjoyable than going to the county fair with Levi tomorrow evening. And even though I really should limit my time with him to the bedroom, I also felt like I deserved this. Keely said have fun. With Levi. What said fun more than a flipping fair?

My life had been a shit-show lately, and I came here to get away. Levi seemed like the perfect antidote to reality. I never turned down a chance for a funnel cake, either.

"Good night, Levi," I said, slipping out the door.

"'Night, Charlie. Sleep well."

I practically ran down the hall, feeling like I was doing

the old college walk of shame out of a guy's dorm room in nothing but his T-shirt and my panties, and it almost made me giggle.

I'd had sex. With a cowboy. It had fit. I'd come. He'd liked it. Wanted more. I'd been wild, and it had been incredible. I couldn't help the grin that spread across my face.

I couldn't wait to tell Keely.

12

EVI

I SPENT the ride into town considering how I'd fuck Charlie next. When I'd first made the arrangement with her, I'd hoped to fuck her out of my system. I'd been a dumbass because I'd been strangely obsessed with her. Sure, she was hot as hell. That had made my dick happy all this time. I'd satisfied her with it, but I'd thought it would fade. Hadn't I?

Well, after the night before, my need for her hadn't faded at all. In fact, it was getting worse. I'd had my head in the game at work today, but I was distracted. Irritable. All I wanted to do was be back at the ranch. With her.

The sheriff job was crimping my style. Messing with my plan to fuck Charlie all I could before she left.

So when I walked in the door of the bunkhouse and found Charlie gone. I was a grumpy fuck. She wasn't in the stable, either. No one was.

I stomped toward the ranch house to find out what the hell was going on.

"Hey Levi, how's it going?" Willow greeted me.

When she'd first come to Cooper Valley, she'd been working undercover for the DEA. Turned out, she was a shifter, had a pretty ginger wolf in her she hadn't even known about. Rob had known she was his mate from the very first sniff, but she'd given him a run for his money. Even had to deal with being shot by a fucking drug mule who'd been our neighbor. Now, they were inseparable. In fact, they were walking up from the barn hand in hand.

"Where's Charlie?" I demanded, forgetting my manners.

For some fucking reason, Rob looked amused. "She went for a ride with Clint and Johnny. What's the emergency?"

Emergency? No fucking emergency.

Okay, yeah, it was close to an emergency. No one should take my human on any kind of field trip without me.

Dammit.

How did she already become *my human* in my mind? I get my dick wet one night, and suddenly, I'm getting attached? I wasn't pussy whipped like Rob or Colton or Boyd. Hell, or even Clint.

I needed to dial it back.

Rob slapped me on the shoulder. "Let's talk," he said and tilted his head toward the ranch house. I followed. He didn't stop until we were settled in his office, Willow peeling off and heading to the kitchen where scents of spaghetti sauce were making my stomach rumble.

"So bad I'm called to the principal's office?" I dropped in a seat as he moved behind his desk.

He smirked, dropped his hat on the hard surface.

"The problem with shifters is their hearing's strong as fuck. It's impossible to talk in private."

"Or do anything else." Yeah, I'd overheard all of the newly mated couples going at it a time or two.

"So, what's up with you and the vet?" he asked, ignoring my reply.

I'd known Rob since the day I joined the pack, looking for a place to settle. His parents had been killed in a car accident the year before, and he'd been as fucked up as me. He was a year older, and at the time, already the alpha. He had a shit ton on his shoulders but had been handling it well. Perhaps that was why he'd welcomed me so readily; he recognized a screwed up teenager when he saw one.

I'd settled into the bunkhouse and been just like Johnny. Learning everything I could and just... living. I'd been free at Wolf Ranch. Everyone was a shifter. No one hid that from each other. From the town, yes, but pack members shifted and ran in the hills to their hearts' content. They weren't shamed. Verbally abused. Forbidden to be themselves.

It had taken a long time to let go of my anger toward my grandparents, how they'd pretty much chained my wolf inside me. Even safe here, when others on the ranch ran with the full moon, I hadn't been able to shift. I never had. Not once. We figured since I'd never shifted before I lived with my mother's family that I probably wasn't able to do so. Maybe it was because I was half-shifter. Still, my wolf made his presence known. Howling when pissed. Prowling when aroused or eager.

Oh, I knew its feelings when it came to Charlie. He wanted her. Just like me.

I realized Rob was staring at me. Waiting. In his usual fashion, he was patient for a response, but I'd gone off on a wild tangent. I ran my hand over the back of my neck.

"Not much," I replied. Charlie and I were close, but I wasn't going to tell him we were fucking. Fortunately, he hadn't been around to overhear us. At least I hoped not.

"Your scents are mingled in the bunkhouse."

So much for secret keeping. Stupid wolf scenting.

I shrugged. "What? It's not like she's my mate."

He looked down at his worn boots. "You have the urge to mark her?"

I frowned. That wasn't possible, a fact which Rob should know. Then again, no one here had given up on my wolf appearing someday. Especially not after Willow, a half-breed like me, shifted for the first time in a life-or-death situation.

"She's not my mate," I repeated. "I would know."

His dark gaze met mine. "Would you?"

It wasn't meant as a dig, but it was hard to keep the anger down. He'd found his fucking mate. So had the other guys. I'd resigned myself to the fact that I probably never would, but it didn't mean it wasn't annoying as fuck to watch them like some kind of made for TV holiday movie.

"It's a two-week thing." I held up my hand. "Fun while she's here. Nothing more. She'll get that horse bred and head back to Colorado."

My wolf howled, not pleased with me saying that aloud. He wanted more with her. So did I, but I wasn't going to go back on our agreement. Charlie had a life in Colorado. A big-time job. She was smart. Successful. And she had family. A grandfather who needed her, who she loved. She couldn't abandon him when it sounded like he needed her the most.

Besides, shifter-human pairings were a disaster. I knew that from my parents' marriage, even though I was surrounded by successful ones. Even if my wolf never manifested, I was still a shifter. I could never, ever live among humans again. Not even for a mate.

"Then let's introduce her to the pack. See if one of the others recognizes her scent. We could use a vet on the ranch."

Without thought, I stood, tipped over my chair in the process, and swiped all the shit from his desk and onto the floor. Things scattered and crashed, but it was my ragged breathing that was the loudest.

Rob didn't move. Didn't act the least bit surprised. Because he'd fucking done it on purpose.

"She's nothing but fun," he said.

"Fuck you," I snarled. I set my hands on his desk, leaned in. Met his gaze head on. "No one touches her. No one breathes her in."

I stormed out of his office, pissed as hell. But all I heard behind me was Rob's calm chuckle.

He was my friend. He was my alpha. He was also an asshole.

13

HARLIE

AFTER THE HORSEBACK ride with Clint and Johnny to show me more of the ranch than the stable and bunkhouse, I walked from the stable out to the pasture where Serafina was grazing. I wanted to check on her, but really, I wanted a spot all alone. My body was sore in all the best ways—and not from the ride the guys had just taken me on. Their ranch was beautiful, and I could see why they were content to be here. I almost had the urge to pick up roots and stay.

It had been a little weird because it had been the most erotic horseback ride I'd had in my life. Well-worked clit kept rubbing on the saddle, reminding me of how much fun Levi and I had the night before. Feeling that way while riding between two other guys, *not* Levi, had made my thoughts extra naughty. The feelings extra intense.

Which reminded me... I pulled my phone out of my

pocket and dialed Keely as Seraphina trotted over to say hello.

"Hey girl," Keely answered.

"The deed's been done." I stroked behind Seraphina's ears to greet her. A smile spread across my face, not sure if it was because I was happy to see my favorite horse or because I'd taken a hot cowboy for a ride.

"Yes! You had sex? With the hot cowboy? Congratulations!" Her enthusiasm over my sex life made me smile.

"Sure did. And it was better than I imagined." The warm breeze ruffled my hair, and I tucked it behind my ear.

"Ooh, tell me everything."

Setting my foot on the bottom rail of the fence, I said, "Let's just say I plan to make up for lost time while I'm here."

She squealed. "So it wasn't just a one-time thing?"

"Our agreement is it's a fourteen-day thing. For the fourteen nights I'm here."

She was quiet for a second. "Oh. My. God. I'm swooning here. That sounds like the title of a movie. Fourteen Nights with a Cowboy."

"Uh, yeah, no. That lacks a ring." I laughed and rolled my eyes.

"Two Weeks in Paradise? Fourteen Nights to Heaven?"

"Oh my God. Please keep your day job." I giggled. Actually *giggled*. And laughing wasn't usually my thing. I might have been as uptight as they said, but now? I felt different. More relaxed. Calmer.

"*Sooo...* how was it?" she wondered.

I sighed, as if that said it all. "Super hot. It started in the stable and then moved to his bed."

"In the stable? Girlfriend, you're leaving stuff out."

"I'm not telling you every dirty detail." I was leaving some of it just for myself.

"Did you sleep with him? I mean sleep-sleep?"

I shook my head, even though she couldn't see. "No, that felt too intimate."

"I know what you mean. You wouldn't want to get attached when this is just a sex thing."

"Right," I said quickly although my stomach dropped to my boots. Why had Keely calling it *just a sex thing* bother me? That was exactly what it was. What I wanted. What I'd validated when I left his room for my own.

And yet, at the same time, that seemed to demean what we actually had.

But now I sounded crazy. We didn't *have* anything but chemistry. There was no relationship here. Nothing more than a wild fling.

I heard a thud and one of Keely's kids break into screams. "Shit, I have to go!" she said.

"Yep. Catch you later." I hung up and tucked my phone back in my pocket.

I patted Seraphina. "What do you think, girl?"

A strong arm banded around my waist, and I gasped. "I know what I think," Levi growled in my ear.

I relaxed, then laughed—it seemed to be a more frequent occurrence today—and laid my head back on his shoulder. He hoisted me off my feet and bit my neck.

"What *do* you think?" I spun in his arms when he set me down, flung my arms around his neck as I looked up at him.

"I think you need to get fucked again." His eyes took on a yellow-ish glow in the fading light.

"Is that right?" I curled my fingers into the hair that stuck out beneath his hat, but couldn't stop smiling.

"Yep. But let's go to the fair first. I have to show off my prowess at the game booths."

I laughed again. "You do not need any fair games to prove your prowess to me."

He growled playfully, then nipped my neck.

I angled my head to the side, so he had more room. I had no idea my skin there was so sensitive. "Will there be food? I'm famished." *And not just for food.*

He pulled back, looked down at me. His smile was affectionate. "Woman after my own heart. Yep. All kinds of food. Barbecue, funnel cakes, freshly churned ice cream— you name it."

"I'm in," I smiled. "Let me just grab a quick shower, and we'll go."

"Deal," he said. "Last one to the showers is a rotten egg."

I laughed and took off running, looking over my shoulder when it seemed he wasn't following. Turned out he was giving me a head start. As soon as I looked, he sped into action, quickly catching up to me and smacking my ass.

"Oh yeah," he rumbled as we kept running. "I'm definitely going to spank that ass some more."

14

EVI

"PICK ONE," I told Charlie. We stood in front of the shoot 'em up booth at the fair. I'd given over my money and shot all the ducks that had moved across the game's backdrop. The toy gun had horrible aim, and there was something sticky on the trigger, but I had to prove to my woman that I could save her from anything. Stupid, caveman thoughts. I didn't need to kill ducks to save her from anyone, and I had a real gun on my hip.

While Cooper Valley was small, the county was vast and people from all over came to enjoy the few days of the fair every summer. Besides the usual 4-H and other kids programs, there were contests for most attractive chickens and pigs, lambs and cows. Pie contests, cherry pit spitting competitions, even a small rodeo. Held over three days, it was always fun. I'd never been as sheriff before, so working the event all day had been different for me. But clocking out and taking it all in with a date... well, it made it a fuck ton more pleasant.

Especially when my date was the woman I'd gotten inside the night before. I knew what she looked like naked. What she looked like when she came all over me. Hell, I was the *only* one who knew what she looked like when she took a dick for the first time.

Mine.

I hadn't seen Charlie this morning before I left, not since she walked out of my room the night before. She'd gone early to the stable for another round of breeding for Seraphina. I'd headed into town to work my shift as sheriff by the time she was finished. Although, knowing her as I did now, she hadn't spent the rest of the day lazing about. That woman worked hard and had a lot on her shoulders. I couldn't make her job any easier or help with anything going on with her grandfather, but I could help her take her mind off of all of it. Gladly. And often.

I'd done a pretty good job of it the night before, and no one had ever considered me to slack at my tasks.

"What should I pick?" An easy smile softened her face. She looked up at all the stuffed animals strung up around the edges of the booth.

I shrugged, enjoying her pleasure. It seemed I wanted to satisfy her in and out of the bedroom, which went beyond the whole two-week thing.

As she decided, the carnival guy took money from a dad with a little boy and handed him one of the game's guns. Finally, Charlie pointed up over my head. "That one."

I glanced up. Froze. A stuffed wolf. "That one?" I asked, stunned.

She nodded. The guy came back our way, and I pointed to the wolf. He used a long stick with a hook on the end and took it down then handed it to Charlie.

"Did you know the gray wolf was introduced back into the wild in Yellowstone twenty-five years ago?"

I raised a brow but said nothing, allowing her to continue.

"They were almost wiped out which meant the ecosystem was out of balance. Their reintroduction returned the balance. They're amazing creatures. So misunderstood."

She tucked the wolf under her arm and stroked the head as if she were a little kid.

I wanted to be stroked like that. My wolf, stuck inside, wanted that too. Real fucking bad. Her words soothed something in me, that she thought we were amazing. That there wasn't tons of information about us. It was all true, but she was talking about the gray wolf, not me. Not anyone at Wolf Ranch.

She looked around. "Do you smell that?"

I frowned, lifted my head to sniff. "What?"

She gripped my arm as if suddenly overcome. "Funnel cakes. I'm dying for one."

I couldn't help but grin as she turned and followed the scent of fried dough. Like a fucking shifter following the scent of his mate.

The sun had set, and the lights from the fair cast a colorful glow over everything. The heat from the hot sun was gone, and it was a perfect Montana summer night. I probably wouldn't have noticed any of that if I hadn't been with Charlie. I was turning sappy with her around, which so wasn't me. Hell, I'd never won a stuffed animal prize for a woman before in my life. Human *or* she-wolf.

I slung my arm around her shoulder as we stood in line for the fried treat, to order and pay. I was... content. Sure, I wanted to get her back in bed and take my time kissing and licking every inch of her, but this wasn't just about sex. Well, not now. Maybe it had been before, but somehow, it had grown into something more. Hell, I was enjoying my time with a woman, with a human, and we had all our clothes on.

I got a few nods, a few hellos since people from town knew me, but I was left to my own devices. Everyone was enjoying themselves, as I was.

Charlie pulled money from her purse which she had slung cross shoulder. I stilled her hand and paid for the treat. "A date, remember?" I asked.

She gave me a smile, then a kiss on the cheek as she was handed the funnel cake on a grease-stained paper plate. She grabbed a metal shaker and sprinkled confectioners sugar all over it.

She couldn't walk and eat, so we found an eating area with a bunch of picnic tables. We sat across from each other as she attacked the dessert. One thing about her, she wasn't a prissy eater. She liked her food.

"Want some?" she asked as she held up a piece. I reached out, took hold of her wrist and ate the bite from her fingers, ensuring to lick some of the sweet sugar off the tips as I did so.

"Not as sweet as you," I said.

My cell rang, and I pulled it from my pocket. "Barnes, what's going on?"

Charlie looked to me as I listened to Barnes, the deputy on shift.

"I've got Tanner Wagner behind the stands at the fair," he said. "Caught him buying E. Has a stash of pills that would set half the high school rolling."

"I'm actually here but in the food area. I'll be right over," I told him.

"Oh, great. I know you're not on shift, but I thought you'd want to know."

"Thanks." I hung up then met Charlie's gaze. "I've got to deal with something over by the rodeo area. A kid with drugs—intent to sell."

Her face lost all the amusement it held just a minute ago. I knew how she felt. Being sheriff was a pain in the ass sometimes, but having a shifter in the ranks would pay off for the pack in the long run. Having someone who knew about our kind without giving up the secret of who we were was important. We never knew when we needed help with the law. Selena Jenkins was a lawyer, but also a shifter, who'd come through for Clint's mate, Becky, last fall. Having someone in the department was even better. I owed it to the pack. Everyone thought I was good enough for the role since I'd been voted into the position from the town council. Still, it seemed I was the only one who still held doubts.

"Do you want me to stay here?" she asked.

I stood, picked up her trash, tossed it in a nearby can. "Nah, this won't take long."

When she came around the table to join me, I took her hand. "Besides, when I'm done scaring the shit out of this kid, I want to take you home. Get you naked again."

Yeah, this wouldn't take long. Not if the look on Charlie's face was any indication of how much she liked my idea of getting her naked.

We headed around to Barnes' squad car at the west end of the fairgrounds. Tanner Wagner, who I pegged around fifteen, stood in handcuffs, slouched against the car, his head hanging. Charlie hung back as I approached.

"What's going on?" I said in my deepest, most intimidating voice.

The kid's head jerked up, and he stared at me with wide eyes. Yeah, he knew who I was.

Barnes held up a ziplock bag containing tiny plastic bags, each with a pressed white pill inside. "Found him with this. There's twenty pills in there."

"Twenty pills." I looked at Barnes, as if I were making conversation with him, and not for the benefit of the kid. "That could get him, what? Five years and up to a hundred-fifty thousand in fines?"

"It would if he were eighteen," Barnes agreed, picking up the conversation smoothly. He was a good deputy and in a few years would make a great sheriff himself. "Still could, if the judge thinks he deserves it."

The kid turned pale, and I was a little worried he might piss himself. Good. If fucking with him now got him scared enough to wet his pants, maybe he was a good kid doing a dumb thing. Maybe this would steer him back onto the right path.

I lasered him with a stern look. "Selling drugs is just plain wrong. I am not exaggerating when I say it will ruin your whole goddamn life. This goes beyond legal consequences, though. Laws are in place for a reason, and they're not just to impede your ability to party with your friends. You know that shit's dangerous, right? What happens if the kid you sell that to dies? You'd be responsible. What if that kid who died was someone you cared about? How would you feel then? This is not something you fuck around with. Not unless you want to write your whole future off right now."

Tanner turned to the side and wretched, losing his lunch in the dirt. I was wrong about pissing himself. Close enough.

Barnes gave me a knowing smirk.

Yep, my work here was done. But the kid still had to face the consequences.

I walked a few paces back toward Charlie and motioned Barnes to come my way. "See if you can find out where he bought it," I said.

"He claims he found it at school." Barnes rolled his eyes at the obvious lie because it was the middle of summer vacation.

"Right. Well, keep working him until his parents come to the station to get him. You might suggest they let him spend the night in the cell to get the full effect of the consequences he's going to be facing."

"Will do." Barnes looked over at Charlie, who stood watching and wringing her hands, as if she were the one in trouble and not Tanner.

I tipped my head her way. "If you'll excuse me, I've got a date."

Surprise flickered over Barnes' face followed by a smile. Hell, I surprised myself. It wasn't like me to publicly announce my interest in a woman. I was usually the *hook up at the bar and never speak of it again* type.

I was outright claiming Charlie in the human way.

And strangely, when I thought about claiming her in the wolf way—a way that wasn't possible for me since my teeth had never once descended in order to bite a mate's neck—my dick got hard.

Which meant it was time for us to go. I adjusted my package.

"Enjoy yourselves," Barnes said.

"Will do. See you tomorrow." I tipped my cowboy hat and walked back to Charlie. "Ready to head back to the ranch?"

She nodded, eyes still wide at what she'd witnessed. Which wouldn't strike me as strange until much, much later.

15

HARLIE

My stomach clenched in a tight knot on the way home. After hearing the dressing down he gave the teenager caught selling drugs, I couldn't stop freaking out.

He'd face up to five years and a hundred-fifty thousand dollars in fines.

The way he'd growled the consequences at the kid, who'd been quaking in his boots at that point, proved he was more than serious. While he'd clearly been trying to scare the kid straight, he'd also meant every word.

I felt as if he hadn't been speaking to the teenager, but to me.

Me, the adult. Me, the adult who was pretty much peddling ridiculous quantities of ketamine, better known as Vitamin K, on the streets. Well, I wasn't on the street corner swapping it for cash, but it was pretty much the same thing.

I was the one who would be facing time behind bars if

anyone found out. I still couldn't believe I'd gotten myself backed into a corner like this with Dax.

A good-looking twenty-something still young enough to think life revolved around partying with his friends, Dax worked in Mr. Claymore's stables. In the hierarchy of the place, he looked more like a street punk than ranch hand, but he was well-liked by everyone. He'd been working there since he was a teen, much longer than me. He was charming —a favorite of everyone, including me, until things went south.

I was so stupid. Collosally stupid. Dax had been his usual charming self—flirty and fun when he'd first approached. I'd known he was too young for me and not serious, but I'd enjoyed the male attention since my sex life had been nil.

I'd smelled marijuana around the stables before but hadn't said anything. It seemed pretty accepted by all the stable hands, especially since it was legal in Colorado, so I went with the flow. Except when they smoked it *in* the stables. That was the biggest fuck no of all. There was no smoking of any kind in that building, and I'd let them all have it when I'd caught them once.

One day, completely out of the blue, Dax had cornered me in my office and asked a bunch of questions about ketamine. Told me he had a friend who'd tried it. He wanted to see what it was like—just once. I told him it was dangerous, and he shouldn't mess around with it. For horses, which was the intentional use for it at the stable, it was as an anaesthetic. I ordered it, kept the clinic stocked. In humans, it was used for the same purposes, but also in other ways. As a date rape drug, for one. To help relax someone. To hallucinate. Lots of possibilities, and Dax wanted to know it all. Maybe minus the date rape part.

"Well, that's why I'm talking to you about it," he'd said. "I mean, you're a doctor. Can you give it to me straight? Like what dose is safe and what's dangerous to make me feel good?"

God. I'd felt uncomfortable immediately. I was an animal doctor. I didn't treat or prescribe medications for humans. His questions weren't tied to working with the horses.

I hadn't liked it. Not at all, but I hadn't wanted him screwing around with his friends and overdosing. Or worse, to harm someone unsuspecting. So I gave him the facts— calculated a safe dosage by his weight and wrote it down for him, so he wouldn't get it wrong, but told him I didn't like it. That it was dangerous. Illegal.

In retrospect, I saw how dumb I'd been. Soooo stupid. I'd written it on a prescription pad like I was dosing him. And he'd gone into the clinic at the stable and taken the supply of ketamine right out from under my nose without me realizing. It wasn't like all meds were locked up.

That was when things had turned ugly.

When I confronted him, he'd shown me a photo of my note on his phone. My handwriting, the proper dosage for him—a human. He told me it was evidence of my abuse of my license and if I didn't order more ketamine—a large quantity—he'd show Mr. Claymore and the police. Tell them I'd been offering him drugs. Drugs that were meant for horses not humans. That I'd been abusing my credentials, my position on the ranch.

This had been a month ago, the same time Pops started really going downhill. I hadn't been thinking straight at the time. I hadn't known what to do, not with Dax, not with Pops. Even now, I honestly wasn't sure Mr. Claymore would believe me and the truth over Dax. This was why I hadn't said anything and done what Dax had wanted. I needed the job. Hell, I needed my vet license I'd worked so hard for. The school debts for it I was still paying off.

Mr. Claymore loved Dax. Everyone did, even though he was a two-faced piece of shit. He was like a chameleon, changing his moods and emotions, his personality to each situation. As for me, I was just the one who kept her head down and spreadsheets up to date. Yeah, I was the upright vet no one really knew much about. I was the newcomer on the job—I'd been there less than nine months. An outsider, by race, gender and my buttoned up personality.

I'd made my second mistake and ordered the ketamine.

That was when I became what he'd said he would accuse me of—a drug dealer. I didn't *deal* the drugs. I didn't stand on a street corner and peddle them. No, I was worse. I got the drugs under the guise of legitimacy.

I swallowed down the ever-present anxiety and looked to Levi in the dark truck, whose eyes were squarely on the road as we cut through the canyon out of town.

"What do you think will happen to that kid?" I asked.

"Who? Tanner?" he asked, glancing at me for a second. "Probably just community service. He's only fifteen. His parents will have to come to the station and pick him up. He'll hopefully get more punishment from them."

I bit my lip. "If he was eighteen, it would really be five years?"

Levi shot me another curious glance. "You interested in law enforcement?"

"Oh! Um, no. I just feel for the kid, you know? Sometimes people get themselves into things without fully understanding the consequences."

People like me, who couldn't figure out how to get out. Maybe Levi would give me some ideas.

"I know." His broad shoulders went up in a big shrug. "But wrong is wrong. That's why I went hard on him back there. Scare him away from the dark side. Today, E. Tomorrow... who the hell knows? Choices he makes now could completely ruin his life. Destroy all his potential for a decent future."

My stomach bunched up even tighter.

"H-how did you get into law enforcement?" I asked. "Did you always want to be a cop?"

Levi considered, like no one had asked him this before. "The people who killed my parents were never brought to justice. I guess that's been sitting on me for the past fifteen years. So when the sheriff's department was short a deputy last year, I decided to give it a go. Rob's wife, Willow, as I told you, came to the area as an undercover DEA agent—that's a long story there—and we'd found out our neighbor had been a big time drug dealer. It didn't sit well with me, you know? I didn't like feeling powerless against the bad shit going down in my valley. The guy was an asshole and was messing with people from the ranch."

Oh God. Levi was going to hate me when he found out what I'd done. He would never understand or be able to forgive.

Neither would Mr. Claymore.

"You just signed up last year, and you're already sheriff?"

"As I said last night, acting sheriff. But yeah, after Sheriff Duncan had his heart attack. He's a good guy. Protected the county for over twenty years. Hard shoes to follow."

Under different circumstances, I would admire Levi for his choice to protect and serve. But now, I found myself on the wrong side of the law. There was more than just the middle armrest between us.

I was a criminal, and he was going to sniff me out.

If I were smart, I'd back out of our arrangement right now. Sever ties and keep my head down. Get Seraphina bred and get back to Colorado. Or should I confess all and offer myself up to the law? Wouldn't I rather it be someone like Levi who arrested me than a stranger back home? In front of everyone I worked with? I wasn't sure if I'd pee my pants or throw up when it happened.

Neither option was appealing.

My thoughts had been circling around this track for weeks now. Tell Mr. Claymore. Turn myself in. Face the consequences and get free of Dax's blackmail.

Only there was Pops to think about. If I lost my license, how would I support us? How would I pay for his medical bills, and if things continued as I expected, some kind of memory care program? Or worse, if I went to jail, who would take care of him? I needed to figure some other way out of this nightmare.

"Shit!" Levi shouted as a border collie ran across the road on three legs, favoring the fourth.

He braked hard and swerved, then pulled over. I gasped, set my hand on the dashboard. The road was seriously dangerous. While he'd said accidents happened in the canyon all the time, I doubt he expected it would be a dog though that might cause us harm.

That dog needed my help.

He put the truck in gear, and we both jumped out. The air was cooler in the canyon, the sound of rushing water from the river that cut through it was loud. And it was black as pitch out. Only the headlights allowed us to see the stray.

"Hey girl," I called, moving slowly, so I wouldn't frighten her away. I held my hands out away from my sides as I assessed her. She stopped and looked over her shoulder at me, panting heavily. Her fur was thick and matted in spots, black with a white nose and paws. I didn't see a collar.

She was probably dehydrated, and judging by her sagging belly, heavily pregnant in addition to being injured.

"Looks like she's about to have pups." I crouched down and held out my hand. "Come here, girl," I said, my voice soft. "I'm going to help you."

———

LEVI

"Where do you want to treat her?" I asked, carrying the injured dog from the truck into the stable. We'd settled her in the truck in the back seat. Charlie sat back there with her, stroking her and reassuring her and making sure she didn't slide around as I drove to the ranch. The rest of the ride, she spoke quietly to the dog, who didn't appear to be all that much of a stray. She wasn't skittish and seemed to know a ride when she had one.

"Right in here, where I have all my equipment," she said, indicating Seraphina's stall.

I gently set the dog on its three working paws, and Charlie squatted down to care for her. Seraphina snorted and shifted her back feet, but didn't crowd.

The injured dog had limped right over to Charlie when she called out on the side of the highway, as if she knew exactly who would help her. Charlie had been magnificent to watch. She clearly adored animals. As closed and guarded as she seemed with humans, this was her element. Kindness and caring radiated from her as she tended to the injured dog. I had to admit, I felt a little jealous of the tenderness she was showing. I wanted her to stroke my wolf, although it wasn't as if I could ever shift to it.

"While I don't have an x-ray machine, it's clear her leg is broken," she said without looking up. "Could you bring me my bag? It's just outside the stall. I'll sedate her to set it and put a cast on."

I brought the bag as she settled the dog on her side and got to work, not seeming to mind that she was sitting in the hay of a stable. When she finished, she stroked the sleeping dog's side.

"How soon do you think she'll give birth?" I asked, squatting down beside her and checking out the dog's swollen belly.

"Based on her size, soon." Charlie's smile lit up her face. "Within a few days, by my guess. Hope Rob won't mind having puppies around, at least until they're old enough to be moved. We can maybe see if she's microchipped."

I met her chocolate gaze, smiled. "Rob won't mind. Who doesn't love puppies?"

The truth was, shifters were mixed about keeping dogs. Some loved them because it was so easy to train them with alpha dominance. Others found it strange to keep a pet from a closely-related species, even if we weren't typical wolves.

Wolf Ranch hadn't had any dogs since I moved here, but that didn't mean they wouldn't keep this one, if we couldn't find her owner. And like I said, who didn't love having pups around?

I smiled to myself, thinking about how much pleasure those puppies would bring little Lizzie and Lily, although they'd enjoy them more when they were a little older.

"I don't want to leave her here unsupervised," she said.

I tipped my head out the stall door. It was late and the last place Charlie should spend the night was in the stable.

Being selfish, I wanted her in my bed, for as long as she'd stay. We had things to do, like me showing her different positions in which to fuck.

I wasn't as altruistic as Charlie, but hell, it was time for her to pay me a little attention. Yeah, I sounded like a whiny fucker.

"I'll carry her up to the bunkhouse. I can get some old blankets. We'll get her settled in my room on the floor. Then we'll get you settled in my bed."

Her eyes widened, and she looked away shyly, but said, "Yes, please."

Fuck, yes.

 HARLIE

"Woman, the dog is asleep and fine. It's my turn for attention."

I knelt by the dog, whom I'd named Shadow, petting her soft fur and feeling her swollen belly. It was Levi's grumbly tone that had me looking over my shoulder at him. He was in bed, his back resting against the headboard. He was shirtless and... stunning. God, this guy wanted me. He'd *had* me and wanted more.

I'd gotten ready for bed first and hadn't paid him much attention after he'd headed to the bathroom.

Perhaps that had been an error on my part.

Slowly, I stood. I wore his T-shirt, the one I'd taken the night before. And nothing else. His gaze raked over my body and settled on my chest where I knew my nipples were hard.

"Are you feeling neglected?" I walked to the bed, then crawled up the length of it to kneel beside him. The sheet was up over his waist, but it did nothing to hide the way it tented from his hard cock.

Gone was the lawman. Gone was the cowboy. He was *all* man and only had eyes for me.

"I was," he said, a pout in his voice.

I laughed. "Well, what *exactly* has been neglected? I don't want you to hurt or ache anywhere," I replied in a— hopefully—sexy voice.

"Oh, doll, there's a place on me that aches something fierce. You'll need to give it special attention."

I liked this playful side of Levi. I'd had his aggressive kisses, his powerful hands. But this? It was... fun.

I leaned in and set my hand on his jaw, kissed him. My lips were gentle, light. I peppered them along his jaw and down his neck, my hands following and sliding over the hard muscles of his shoulders, chest and abdomen. I felt them tense and harden beneath my palms. He was hot to the touch, his skin soft, the smattering of hair on his chest darker than on his head.

I licked, then sucked the flat disks of his nipples, just as he'd done with mine. Glancing up, I found his gaze on me. Watching.

He didn't touch me, just let me explore.

"Okay?" I asked.

He huffed out a rough laugh. "Fuck, doll. Anything you do I'll love."

With one hand, I worked the sheet from his hips. Lower and lower still, so his cock bobbed free. He wasn't wearing anything. And he wasn't the least bit modest. With his body, there was nothing to be modest about. He should be in one of those cowboy calendars.

"Do you hurt here?" I asked, lowering my head and

kissing the crown of his cock. I licked my lips, tasted his salty essence.

He hissed, and his hips bucked involuntarily.

"It's hurting to get in you again," he replied. The words were like rocks rubbing together. Rough and tumbled. "I didn't think it would be your mouth this go, but fuck, doll. Lick it. Yes, like that. Such a good girl, learning to suck dick. Oh shit..."

He didn't say anything after giving me a little instruction because I'd taken him deep, as deep as I could go, which was all the way to the back of my throat. He was so big and thick... more than I imagined. I couldn't breathe, so I pulled back a little, paused, then took a breath through my nose and tried again. I'd never done this before, but I'd seen porn. I knew what to do, or I hoped I did.

I hollowed out my cheeks as I lifted off him, sucking hard.

"Holy fuck, you don't have a gag reflex."

I wasn't aware I didn't have one, but I assumed that was a good thing in this case. Licking my lips, I looked up at him again. His jaw was clenched, the tendons in his neck corded. His hands gripped the bedding as if he was trying to keep himself from attacking.

"Is that a good thing?" I wondered.

One second, I was leaning over his throbbing dick, the next Levi flipped me onto my back and loomed over me. "Good?" he breathed. "Any better, and I'd really be hurting."

"I thought you liked it." I stared up at him, confused. Why would he want me to stop if I was doing it right?

"If I liked it any more, I'd have come down your throat faster than I want. That's not how it's going to work tonight. Tonight I get to play. Find out how many times I can get you off."

"That sounds good and all, but I want..." I couldn't say it, and I glanced away.

"What? Tell me what you want."

His finger tipped my chin back, so I met his gaze.

"I want your dick. In me. I... I liked that a lot." I had. While I'd imagined kissing and making out, being touched and stuff by a guy, what I'd imagined having a dick in me would be like and the real thing were two different things. There was no comparison between Levi and a dildo. I'd be throwing the one in my drawer out when I got home. Until then, I wanted to take Levi's for a spin. Or two.

A slow grin spread across his face. "Oh, you'll get dick, don't you worry."

He moved back to pull me up and help me out of the T-shirt. As I raised my arms, I glanced down at Shadow, who was still asleep.

Levi turned my face back with a finger. "If you're distracted by a sleeping dog, then I'm not doing this right."

I blinked then gave him a sheepish smile. "Sorry."

"Since you like things all organized and the likes although I don't have a spreadsheet for this kind of thing... here's what's going to happen. An agenda for our fucking. Ready?"

I grinned, nodded. He sooo understood me, and that made my heart flip.

His hand slid down my neck and to my nipple. He flicked it once then circled it. "I'm going to play with these babies and see if you can come from just nipple play alone. Then I'm going to spread your gorgeous thighs and settle myself between them. You're going to come from a good tongue fuck. Then I'm going to find your g-spot and see if you make it ten seconds before you come again. Got all that?"

I nodded then clenched my core.

"Then, maybe then, I'll give you my dick. I might start with you on your back, but I have no doubt, you'll be flipped onto all fours and fucked from behind. Maybe I'll bend you over the bed to take you even harder. If you're a good girl and scream my name when you come, I might show you a few other fun ways to fuck. You up for all that?"

I glanced down between us, took in how hard he was, how the skin was stretched taut, the vein that went up the length bulging with blood.

"You are," I countered.

He grabbed my ankle and tugged me down, so I was flat on my back. In less than two seconds, his mouth was on my breasts. He flicked his tongue over one nipple as he pinched the other. I squirmed at the mixture of sensations—one gentle, one firm. He bent and took my nipple into his mouth, sucking it. I instantly felt the answering tug between my legs. I arched up, head thrown back, legs moving restlessly behind him.

"Touch yourself," he commanded. "Show me how you make yourself come while I'm working these nipples."

It felt so naughty. Hedonistic. But I did it—because that was why I was here, wasn't it? To indulge? To de-stress? I slid my fingers between my legs. My lady bits were flooded with arousal, slick and swollen. It was amazing how the female body changed to prepare for sex.

I moaned when he moved to the other nipple. I didn't even mean to do it, but one of my fingers sank into my heat up to the knuckle. I pushed my palm over my clit as I dipped into my juices, undulating my palm and fingers as I bucked my hips.

"That's right, Doc. Get yourself hot for me."

I moaned louder.

"You gonna come before I even get my mouth down there? Can you?"

It was like a challenge. I didn't have to hold out. He was daring me to come. I let my eyes roll back in the sockets, opened my mouth and let out a guttural tone, "Uhn."

"Can you, Doc?"

"Uhn."

"Show me."

I worked myself as I did in the past when I was all alone, but it was hotter now knowing Levi was watching me. Seeing how I liked it.

It didn't take long. I came on a breathy moan. My muscles squeezed and pulsed as my heart tapped out a rapid beat against my ribs. It felt so good, so satisfying. And this was just the beginning of our love-making.

I caught my breath as the orgasm passed, still working my fingers.

Levi raised onto his forearms and claimed my mouth in a hard, possessive kiss. I lifted my hips to meet his and felt his very solid erection. He groaned against my lips. "Not yet, beautiful. I still have another step on the agenda."

My eyelids fluttered as he crawled down between my legs and made good on his promise. In fact, he went through every item on his agenda before he let me sleep. In his bed.

HARLIE

TWO DAYS PASSED. While I focused on my work with Seraphina and all the reports and phone calls with the staff back in Colorado, I was in a sexual haze. I patted the animal's flank as I put the portable ultrasound away. "Guess both of us are getting some action this trip," I murmured.

Seraphina's ear flicked, the only indication she'd heard. Not that I'd expected her to ask for every hot detail like Keely.

I'd lost track of the number of orgasms Levi had given me. I should have made a spreadsheet of that, tracking the hows and whens of each one, so I could put the pretty pie chart on the wall when I got home.

He'd been on shift both days as sheriff, but Levi was an attentive, thorough and fun lover when he got home. All my hangups and worries about being with a guy diminished every time he winked or smiled or kissed me. When he was deep inside me, whether it was bent over the arm of the couch in the bunkhouse or a quickie in the empty stall next to Seraphina's, I didn't think about anything. Not about being overheard or found. Not about my work. Not about what things with Levi meant because we'd clearly delineated this was a sex-only fourteen-day relationship. Not about Pops. Or Dax. Or anything.

While I had a feeling Clint and the others on the ranch knew we were into each other, they didn't comment. Thankfully, Clint was content to head home to his wife and daughter at the end of the day. As for Johnny, he came early and did his work but left well before sundown. Levi had told me Boyd and Audrey were staying in town because Audrey had shifts at the hospital this week. I didn't know the details about that arrangement, but they weren't around.

Everyone was busy. So was I, with Levi.

I liked him. I felt comfortable around him. I felt like I could be me, and that said a lot. It was crazy and fun and everything I'd ever wanted. Yet it was a big problem. This was a fling. Two weeks. Nothing more. He was supposed to teach me about sex and to punch my V-card. He'd done both.

He was a thorough, attentive teacher, and I was a very eager pupil. My pussy tingled from all the attention he'd given it and craved more.

What we had was real, but it had an expiration date. I had about a week to go, and I'd be packing up Seraphina and heading back to Claymore's. I'd be leaving Wolf Ranch and Levi behind.

This was what he wanted. He'd only offered two weeks. Nothing more. I couldn't get any silly notions that he'd be thinking beyond that time. I was a fling to him. He hadn't said otherwise, and if I asked him, I'd be the clingy, needy woman.

I wasn't that. Never that.

Seraphina nickered, and I smiled at her. "You're the love 'em and leave 'em type, aren't you? You don't have any issue with riding off into the sunset, leaving poor Eddison to find another mare."

She tossed her head as if agreeing.

My cell chimed, indicating a text. My heart jumped into my throat because it was either Keely or Dax. I gave Seraphina one more pat then retrieved the cell from my bag.

"Shit." It wasn't Keely.

Dax: The shipment still hasn't arrived.

I stared at the text. Honestly, I was relieved he didn't have his grubby hands on the stuff. That meant it wasn't being sold. But it also meant I was still on the hook and got annoying texts.

I stared up at the rafters of the stable, wondering what the hell happened to my life. I was screwing cowboys and peddling drugs. I'd gotten him exactly what he wanted. It wasn't my fault someone was diligent and locked the drugs away. Still, Dax wasn't reasonable.

Me: OK

I had no idea what else to put. I wanted to type in so many things. "So?" or "Fuck you." or "Deal."

He responded right away.

Dax: You better B bringing the other batch with U. Or else.

Tears filled my eyes instantly. There was no escape. He wanted the ketamine however I could get it. I was too far into this now. I should've gone to the police from the start. Shoulda, woulda, coulda.

"Charlie!" Clint shouted.

I wiped my eyes and dropped my cell back into my bag.

"In here!" I called back, then stuck my head out Seraphina's stall.

He was coming my way at a fast clip, but there was a smile on his face, cutting through my instant worry. "I think you're about to be a momma."

I instantly thought of Levi and the condoms we'd used. They'd worked, as far as I knew, and I was on the pill.

"Shadow seems to be in labor." He opened the stall door for me. "Come on."

We walked together to the bunk house, our steps quick. From Levi's bedroom, we'd moved Shadow to a comfortable corner in the main room where others could come in and check on her. We'd shifted the couches so she was enclosed with the wall on one side, the backs of the couches on two others so she felt like she had a pseudo-nest. She had the old blankets beneath her, so she was comfortable. By the time we got to her, two puppies had slid out already.

I put my finger to my lips so Clint stayed quiet. Shadow knew what to do, and I would only mess with the process. I'd only help if needed. After another was delivered and Shadow was licking off the membrane, I looked to Clint who watched the process leaning over the back of the couch.

"Got a heating pad around?" I whispered.

He nodded, then went to retrieve it, and I tucked it beneath the blankets so the babies would stay warm. Clint took the cord and plugged it in.

All in all, there were eight pups total. Some were all black, the others black and white. They were tiny and perfect and nursing from a proud Shadow.

By dinnertime, news had spread of the new ranch babies, and everyone had stopped by to visit.

"I agreed to board one extra horse not nine dogs," a large

cowboy teased, adjusting his hat on his head. A beautiful redhead scooted around from behind him and dropped to her knees in front of the puppies.

"Oh. So cute!" she gasped.

I scrambled to my feet and brushed off my jeans.

"I'm Rob Wolf, owner of this ranch." He gave me a small smile and held out his hand. "Sorry I haven't come by to introduce myself before now."

"Charlie Banbrook."

"You're not a man," he said with a wink.

"That's what everyone tells me," I countered. "Nice to meet you. Thanks for having me and Seraphina. The dogs I didn't bring, but *surprise!*" I opened my fingers in jazz hands and shook them.

He chuckled then tipped his chin toward the redhead. "This is my wife, Willow."

Willow. Right. The DEA agent.

I started sweating, as if she might somehow sniff me out just being in close proximity. She looked at me and grinned. "This is so much better than picking out fencing."

I remembered that Marina had said they'd gone to Billings to man shop.

"Nice to meet you." I joined Willow on the floor by the pups.

"We're keeping one." Willow stroked Shadow's ears. It wasn't a question, it was a firm statement, like she dared Rob to disagree.

I looked over my shoulder at her husband when she didn't.

He shrugged. "Happy mate, happy fate."

It was a strange variation of the "happy wife, happy life," and both Clint and Willow looked askance at him.

"What?" He lifted his shoulder again. "It's true. You went

fencing shopping which made me happy," he said to Willow. "Now you get to pick a puppy which makes you happy."

Willow smiled at him and shook her head as if he were an idiot. But I didn't think she'd argue since he agreed to the puppy.

"I checked Shadow for a microchip, but she doesn't have one," I said aloud, figuring everyone would want to know. "I also called the local animal shelter to tell them we had her, but they hadn't had a dog matching her description reported missing."

"Well, we'll keep Shadow, for sure," Willow said. "But I definitely want one of her puppies as well."

"Becky wants one, too," Clint said.

"So do I," Marina piped in. "I know Boyd will want one, too. For Lizzie.

"Somehow I have a feeling this place is going to overrun with dogs before this is all over," Rob said ruefully, but he wore an indulgent smile.

"Sorry," I said, mock cringing.

"No, we're so grateful you found Shadow and fixed her broken leg. Another day out in that canyon, and she could've died," Clint said.

It was true, and I didn't like to think of what could have happened.

"And these puppies—" Willow clapped a hand over her mouth, horrified.

"Well, it didn't happen," I said quickly. "She's going to be fine, and the puppies all seem healthy."

"Hey, looks like you all are having a party without me." The sound of Levi's deep rumble sent my heart flip-flopping. I looked over my shoulder at him. His gaze wasn't on the puppies but directly on me. He walked straight over, crouching down and resting his hand on my back. "What do we have here?"

I beamed proudly, like I was the mama. "Eight little wiggle-pups."

He grinned. "Wiggle-pups. That's cute." He still had barely looked at the puppies. Instead, he studied my face, that look of fascination I sometimes saw on him clearly in place.

I honestly didn't know what I'd done to warrant such attention from him. There was nothing special about me. Nothing different or more beautiful than the next woman. And yet, he seemed to think there was.

"Well, I don't know about you all, but looking at puppies makes me hungry," Levi said. Totally ridiculous because he hadn't even *looked* at the puppies.

"Being *alive* makes you hungry," Marina teased. She looked at me. "I swear to you, these guys eat more than a bear storing up for winter."

Levi scoffed. "Bears eat fish and blueberries. We eat red meat."

Marina laughed. "Don't worry. I took some steaks out of the freezer this morning. There's plenty of red meat for all of you carnivores." She glanced at me. "How about you? Hungry?"

"Yeah, she eats meat," Levi said.

I'm not sure if he meant it to be a double entendre, but Clint and Rob choked a little and looked away to hide smiles.

I tried to ignore the heat in my face. "I would love some steak. That is, if you have enough." Even though Marina expected me to eat with them at every meal, I always asked to make sure I wasn't imposing on their family time.

"Of course, we do. Rob, if you'll fire up the grill, I'll take care of the rest of it." She held out a hand and looked at me. "Please don't go thinking I cook because I'm the woman and these fat-heads can't feed themselves. They're actually quite capable. As I told you the other morning, I just love cooking. Baking, especially."

"I enjoyed your home-baked hamburger buns the night I arrived. Delicious. And the cinnamon rolls." My mouth watered just remembering. "I'll go get cleaned up for dinner."

"I'll help," Levi murmured in my ear, making my pussy clench.

Damn. I liked being at Wolf Ranch way too much. Everyone was so nice. Easy going. They were like a team, a family. Well, they were. Most of them anyway.

Worse than liking this place, I liked *Levi* way too much.

We had a deal—two weeks of pleasure—and then I left.

But I hadn't counted on this. On feeling like I was one of their big extended family. On liking it so much.

On having puppies. God, what could be more sappy than puppies?

I hadn't counted on falling in love.

Shit.

Was I falling in love?

That was definitely not part of the plan. Not in two weeks, and I hadn't even been here half that. Was it because I was new to relationships that I made sex out to be more than it was? It was supposed to be just sex.

But it wasn't *just* sex. Sure, I had nothing to compare it to, but I knew. This wasn't normal. The connection, the chemistry Levi and I shared was... more.

As I looked to Levi, I realized I needed to pull back now because every day I fell deeper would make it harder when I had to leave.

Because I was. Not only did I have to get back for Pops, but Dax was only going to remain barely patient for so long. If I didn't deliver the ketamine, either at Mr. Claymore's or bringing it back to Colorado with me, he'd do something. I didn't know what, but it wasn't going to be good.

And that would mean I was in even deeper. In even more trouble. That meant a bigger betrayal for Levi if he found out what I really was.

And with that thought, the feeling of contentment slipped away.

Or at least it tried to, but halfway to the stairs Levi tossed me over his shoulder and carried me to the shower where he ensured I quickly forgot everything.

HARLIE

"You guys go outside and grill. Leave us to the girl talk."
Marina shooed the men out the back door of the big ranch
kitchen.

I guessed on Wolf Ranch it took about forty minutes to
produce a party. In the time since Marina said she took
steaks out of the freezer, the big ranch house had filled with
people. Most of them I'd met before, but there were a few
new ones. No one knocked. Everyone was loud. Boisterous
and friendly.

Rand, Clint's younger brother, showed up along with
Nash, his best friend. Maybe a couple others. I still hadn't
put them all together. Who was with whom and all that. As
for names, I'd have to make name tags to get them all right.

When the men obeyed Marina and traipsed outside, I
was left in the large kitchen with her, Audrey, Willow and

Becky, Clint's wife. Audrey and Becky both sat in chairs at the table with newborns in their arms. Becky's baby, Lily, nursed noisily. Marina and Willow were busy preparing food at the central island.

Feeling awkward, I made faces at Lizzie, Audrey's baby. "Do you want to hold her?" she asked, pushing her glasses up her nose.

I was a hard core introvert, not much of a people person, but I was a baby person. They were so soft, so tiny. So snuggly.

"Yes, please," I admitted, scooting out a chair to sit beside her. Babies were like animals—totally innocent. Always themselves. No agenda. I took the chubby infant and cradled her in the crook of my arm where I could continue raising my eyebrows and smiling big.

"How old is she?" I wondered.

"Five months," Audrey replied. "She'll be sitting up on her own soon."

"So how's the breeding going?" Willow asked, looking up from slicing tomatoes.

I knew she meant Seraphina, and yet my thoughts instantly went to Levi. Yeah, if women paid a stud for breeding, he would fetch top dollar.

"It's good. According to her hormone levels, implantation has already taken place. I'm just going to watch and make sure the levels keep doubling every day."

"That's great! But you still better stick around a while to be sure, right?" Marina asked with an impish expression on her face. "In case she needs a little more time with her *stud*?" She turned and waggled her brows.

My cheeks got hot, and I looked down at Lizzie who had her hand stuffed in her mouth.

Audrey's gaze sharpened. "Ooh, is there something going on I should know about?"

All the women in the room turned to stare at me. I flushed. "Um..."

"Yay! There is, isn't there?" Marina sounded triumphant.

"Wait—with whom?" Becky demanded. She lifted Lily up onto her shoulder to burp her.

"Levi!" Willow crooned, her eyes alight with something akin to glee.

Becky gasped. "Levi! Oh my God. And Clint was worried he was going to be bent out of shape about sharing the bunk house."

"He wasn't too bent out of shape," I admitted, my body still relaxed and languid from the orgasm he gave me in the shower before we walked over.

"Aw, that makes me so happy," Becky said. "Levi's such a great guy. He's quiet but completely reliable and trustworthy. Hard worker."

"And loyal," Willow added. "Rob said from the moment Levi arrived on Wolf Ranch, he's been one hundred percent attached to it. Even now with his new duties as sheriff."

"I'm only here for another week," I said quickly, suddenly feeling like I was on one of those matchmaker shows. Not that I watched reality shows. I didn't have time for TV.

Besides, knowing Levi would never leave Wolf Ranch didn't do much to make me believe we had a chance beyond these two weeks. I had Pops at home in Colorado. I couldn't leave him.

"Right, of course," Becky said, but they all kept watching me with avid curiosity. I hated being the focus of attention, even as nice and welcoming as they all were.

"So does he talk more in private?" Becky asked.

"Yeah, does he? He's usually the guy sitting quietly in the corner around here," Willow said.

"Um, he talks some." He used his tongue more for other things when we were together, though. But he'd divulged some of his secrets to me—his parents' death and the lack of justice for it. Being raised by stifling grandparents who blamed his dad. It was no wonder he felt attached to this ranch, the first home he had after all that trauma. I felt welcome, and I'd only been here a few days.

And these people... they were kind. I could feel it.

Like the sweet baby staring up at me and smiling, they were unpretentious. Solid. Good people.

The vibe was one hundred percent different from Mr. Claymore's ranch. The people here were more themselves than anyone I knew in Colorado. Even I felt almost comfortable here. Like I didn't have anything to prove. Not as a woman, a person of color or a professional.

My opinions and boundaries were respected. Not that there were epic issues—besides Dax—at Claymore's. But it was a working ranch. Literally that. Everyone was there because they received a paycheck. Everyone at this ranch, while receiving a living wage, *lived* here. This wasn't just a workplace, but a home.

"Well, any chance you'll have to come back? Bring another horse here to breed with our studs?" Marina asked.

"Not my stud," Willow said, and we all laughed.

I shrugged, turned Lizzie so she sat up and faced me, my hands tucked under her armpits. I jiggled my leg, so she bounced a little. "I don't know. It could probably be arranged."

I wanted to. I desperately wanted to know that next week

wouldn't be goodbye with Levi. That there'd be a *see you later* instead.

But that was crazy.

I had a job and Pops. And even if Levi wasn't running for sheriff, he was totally attached to Wolf Ranch. There was no possibility for us to be together.

Dammit.

———

LEVI

OH SHIT.

When I walked in and found Charlie with Lizzie in her arms, something strange and twisty happened in my chest.

What was it?

Fuck. *Longing?*

I'd seen Audrey with Lizzie and had my first—*I want Charlie to have my babies* moment. That had been in my imagination. Now Charlie was holding a baby. I didn't have to imagine what she'd look like with an infant in her arms.

I wanted that. I'd sat back and watched almost all my best friends mate over this past year.

Boyd. Colton. Rob. Clint.

I hadn't been jealous. I hadn't even been sure I wanted what they had. I didn't have the biology of the wolf driving me to mate before I was too old. Or at least, mine was suppressed.

Sure, I'd hoped I'd find my mate. And I'd definitely pictured mating a she-wolf—never a human.

But looking at that sweet softness in Charlie's face as she made baby-talk to Lizzie had my heart lurching.

I wanted that.

Fuck—I wanted that with her.

This was more than fourteen nights. It was way more than sex. Charlie and I fit. I was falling in love with her— everything about her. Her over-active mind and workaholism. The way her walls came down when we were in private. How I felt as big as a mountain when I made her laugh. When I made her come.

How I felt was a pretty damn big problem considering she was leaving in a week.

I walked over and slid an arm loosely around her waist, joining her in pulling faces at Lizzie.

"First puppies, now babies. I think I'm on cute overload," Charlie said, smiling up at me under her black lashes.

"Wait until Seraphina has that colt. It's going to be one very beautiful baby horse."

Charlie's smile was easy—so much quicker than when she first arrived. "I know! I'll have to send pictures." Then her smile faltered as if she, too, was contemplating us being apart.

Knowing it didn't seem right.

"I might have to come visit. Check out Eddison's offspring in person," I said, but I knew it wasn't true. That just wasn't done. Not with a high-paying client like Claymore. We weren't friends. I couldn't just show up at his ranch to "visit" our stud's offspring. That would be unprofessional. "Okay, I guess that would be weird," I admitted aloud.

Charlie's smile returned. "You want to hold her?" she asked, offering the baby.

Honest truth? In the few months since both these two babies arrived at the ranch, I hadn't held one of them.

Hadn't really felt it was something I was missing, either.

Course, it was hard to get the babies away from their overprotective fathers and their doting mothers and aunts.

"I'd love to," I answered honestly, accepting the little bundle of sweetness. "Hey there, Lizzie-loo," I murmured, holding under her armpits and bringing her eye level.

Her tiny face split into a gargantuan smile, tongue extended, feet kicking.

"Look at you. You're so little."

"You won't say that when she screams," Boyd said, walking up behind me and leaning in to steal his daughter's smile. "The baby has a set of lungs on her, let me tell you."

Charlie laughed. "That's good. That means she can communicate her needs."

"Yep. Loud and clear on every dissatisfaction," Boyd chuckled, taking the baby from me and holding her straight over his head. She laughed and gurgled her pleasure. I had her about ten seconds before Boyd took her away. I had to laugh at how the tiny girl had her dad wrapped around her finger. I could only imagine what he'd be like in fifteen years. Hell, all of us men on the ranch would be on vigilant patrol.

I pulled Charlie's back against my front, wrapping my arms around her from behind. I wanted to tell her how much I wanted to put a baby in her belly. Plant my seed and watch it grow. See her carrying our beautiful angel instead of Boyd's and Audrey's.

But we weren't there. And I really didn't see us getting there, no matter how appealing the idea felt.

No, Charlie was leaving, and I had to stay.

Or did I?

Fuck. Was I really considering living amongst humans again? Mating one?

That was crazy. I'd only known Charlie a few days.

And yet, the thought didn't make my wolf twist and rage the way he usually did when I remembered living with my grandparents. Or even as he had a week ago, thinking I had to share the bunkhouse with a human.

Huh.

Maybe this thing could be possible... Maybe?

19

HARLIE

"You're still the big mama here," I said to Seraphina the next day, patting her nose and rubbing her flank. "Just because we have eight cute little puppies doesn't mean you're not going to have the prettiest foal ever." I crooned to the horse, who snuffled and nudged me with her nose. "I'm not sure who the baby daddy is for those pups, but I can tell you, Eddison is a stud."

I smiled.

"Literally," I added. A stud horse whose job was to knock up unsuspecting mares across the country.

I smiled and fed her some sugar cubes.

My bubble of happiness over seeing the puppies being born—and at having a guy of my own, at least for a short time—popped when my cell rang.

I grabbed it from my bag, saw that it was Dax. I also saw

that he'd called before. Not once or twice, but over and over. I'd missed them all tending to Shadow and then dinner with everyone. I had to answer because I knew he wouldn't stop, and I didn't want to talk to him back at the bunkhouse later when Levi was around.

Besides, I didn't know how unhinged he really was.

"Hello?" I asked, even though I knew all too well who had called.

"*Hello-o,*" he snarled in a sarcastic, expectant way.

I winced.

"When you getting back here?" For a really smart guy, he spoke like an idiot.

"Next week." I wasn't going to share more than that.

"Did you get the goods?"

I squeezed my eyes shut. "No. I told you I ordered it. You saw the invoice. I also told you I don't control shipping."

"I control you. You show up without the K, and you're fucked."

"It's on order."

"I'll be waiting." He clicked off.

I dropped my cell in my lap, my head into my hands. What was I going to do?

My cell rang again, and I jumped. It wasn't Dax, but Mrs. Vasquez.

"Hi there," I said, trying to calm my heart and even out my voice.

"Did I catch you at a bad time, dear?" she asked. I could hear the worry in her voice.

"No. What's up?"

"I know you're busy, but something happened with your grandfather."

I popped to my feet. "Is he all right?" I walked out of

Seraphina's stall and paced the long central corridor of the stable.

"He's fine. He was trying to make lunch earlier. Heating up gravy on the stove."

"Oh, God," I said, setting my hand on my forehead.

"He forgot about it, and it began to burn, setting off the smoke detectors. I heard it next door and went over. We got the place aired out, no worries there. He was agitated and angry. I think he was a little ashamed of himself realizing what he'd done."

I blinked back tears, mentally seeing Pops frustrated in himself. Ruining something as simple as heating leftovers would have bothered him.

"We had grilled cheese, and he settled in with his book. I made dinner and took some to him, so he didn't cook tonight."

"Thank you, Mrs. Vasquez." I leaned against a wall with my forearm, set my forehead on it. Shut my eyes. "I don't know what I'd do without you."

"I think it's time, dear. Time to consider someone to stay with him during the day at least."

"You're probably right. I'll see about it when I'm back, if you're okay keeping an extra close eye until I'm back."

"Good, and no problem. I'll watch out for him."

"I'll check in with you tomorrow. And thank you."

She hung up, and I stood there, thinking. Hard. Too hard.

"Hey, doll."

I jumped at Levi's words. He held his hands up. "Sorry. I thought you heard me come in."

Shaking my head. "It's okay. I'm... distracted." I reached down and grabbed an antacid from my bag, popped it in my mouth.

"What has been going on?" he asked. He pulled me into his arms, and I let him. The feel of him hugging me close, of his chest beneath my cheek, felt safe. As if things weren't so bad.

Yet they were.

He'd stayed on the ranch all day, but he and Colton had gone off somewhere to do something... I wasn't exactly sure. A patched roof or something. I hadn't seen him since I'd rolled out of his bed. Yeah, *his* bed. I pretty much gave up on the whole separate beds thing.

"Ultrasound tests show follicle growth, so it's my guess we're close to ovulation, but... whatever. Seraphina's fine," I told him.

"I wasn't really asking after the horse, but I'm glad that's going well." He tipped my chin up, studied my face. "Want to go for a walk? With the rain clouds gathering, it's shaping up to be a beautiful sunset."

A walk. Such a simple pleasure, but one I almost never allowed myself. Not unless someone else invited me. It was stupid how hard I worked.

"That sounds great."

He looped an arm around my shoulders and led me out of the stable and past the main house until we hit a path that seemed to lead up the mountainside. The path was dusty, but the field was sprinkled with yellow and blue wildflowers.

"Where are we going?" I asked.

Levi pointed up to a ridge. "There's a beautiful lookout up there."

I tipped my chin to look in the direction he indicated. "Sounds great."

We walked side by side in silence for about fifteen

minutes until we arrived at the top of a hill. A small plateau with a stunning view of the entire ranch.

"Up here." Levi beckoned me over to a giant boulder, which he helped me climb. I gasped when I reached the top. The valley was laid out below us like a green carpet.

"It's incredible," I breathed.

"I like to come up here when I need some perspective on things," he said. "Sometimes just getting outside, away from buildings and people and structure, makes all the difference."

"I can see that."

I could. My problems didn't feel quite so big anymore. Not when I could feel how much bigger nature was.

"So what had you worked up back there?" he asked, his voice calm and almost soothing. There was no playful tone to it. He was serious. He really wanted to know.

I sighed. There was so much I wanted to share, to tell him. I picked one. One I thought he might understand the most. "It's hard to be away from my grandfather. I have the next door neighbor looking in on him while I'm gone, but I guess that wasn't enough. She called a little while ago to tell me the fire alarms had gone off at the house because he'd forgotten about heating leftovers on the stove. It burned."

"Oh shit." His hand settled low on my back.

"I know." I blinked rapidly, fighting back the tears I'd never allowed myself to cry. "It's hard to watch people you love deteriorate mentally."

"I'll bet." He tugged me in against his chest, and I allowed his strength to envelop me.

I loved the way it felt to be with him. So safe. Cared for. Admired. No one had made me feel this way before. And here we were alone, as if we were in this bubble. And yet, I was talking about my life problems, something that was happening elsewhere.

"You have a lot of responsibility on your shoulders," he said. "And you take it all so seriously."

"I have to." I pulled back far enough to look up at him. His blue gaze was so deep, as if bottomless, as if I could see into him. As if he knew me. Understood. But could he? I held so much back. Had such a big, awful secret.

"Of course, you do."

He kissed my temple. "How about you let me help you forget it all for one night?"

I frowned. "What do you mean?" My problems weren't going away, and I thought about *everything*.

He stroked my hair back. "Is there anything you need to do for your grandfather tonight?"

I thought about it. "No. Mrs. Vasquez said she'd keep extra careful watch. He's probably watching his shows or reading now. I don't want to stir up anything now."

"What about for Seraphina or Shadow?"

"Seraphina's set, and Shadow just needs to go out to do her business. I'll need to give her some water. Clint fed her a little while ago."

"Other than that?" he asked, helping me off the boulder. He held out a hand as I hopped down.

God, he was so calm, so patient. So... nice.

"That's it," I said.

His arm curled around my waist, and he led me back to the path down to the ranch. "Good, then you're going to be tied up with me."

I paused in the middle of the trail. "What do you mean?"

"Just that." He smiled, crossed his arms over his broad chest. He had on his usual jeans and T-shirt for the ranch although I liked him just as much in his sheriff's uniform. I had to admit, it got me hot. Women always said a man in uniform was hot, and I couldn't argue. "You're going to be tied up. There will be nothing you have to do or can do because you'll be my prisoner. And I'm going to have my wicked way with you."

Oh my.

20

EVI

THE ONE THING I'd learned about Charlie was that she was ridiculously smart. That brain of hers worked all the time. Even when she was sitting still, she was thinking about something. There was a saying about a brain being like tabs on a computer browser. Well, Charlie had about fifty open at once.

I couldn't blame her. Being sheriff made me juggle all kinds of complaints and issues at once. Thankfully, the county was pretty peaceful, and we had more issues with natural disasters than human ones. Charlie, though, had lots on her plate. Between her work and her grandfather, that was plenty.

I wanted to help her, to shoulder some of that load, but really, I couldn't. I wasn't a vet. I had barely any knowledge in animal husbandry, and her boss was expecting an impregnated mare upon her return. As for her grandfather, I couldn't make the old guy any better. I couldn't visit with him and ensure he was safe, that he didn't burn any more food. He lived five hundred miles away.

The only thing I could do was give Charlie a break. A mental one. Whenever I got her beneath me, she gave over to our actions. She gave in to my commands although I wasn't all that bossy between the sheets. She let go, forgot. It was a treasured gift that she trusted me so much that she didn't have to think, didn't have to do anything but feel.

I doubted she even knew how much of a gift that was.

I could give her more of that, and the best way to do it, the best way I could think of for someone who just needed to hand everything over was to tie her up.

I hadn't been lying to her about my intentions.

All she had to do was lie there and come.

When I shut the bedroom door behind us, she turned to face me. She tipped her chin up and met my gaze. "This tying up thing, it's not like calf roping, like in the rodeos, right?"

I couldn't help but laugh. "Calf roping ties the legs together. I want your legs spread *wide* apart."

Her mouth fell open as she caught my drift.

"Doll, stop thinking."

She pursed her lips in reply.

I stepped toward her, cupped her face. Kissed her. "Do you have any idea how beautiful you are?"

Her gaze skittered away.

"Do you have any idea how beautiful you are going to be with these around your wrist?"

I dropped one hand, grabbed the handcuffs off my utility belt.

"Oh my God, it's like every woman's fantasy."

I couldn't help but grin. "I know I am."

She smacked me on the arm.

"You okay with this? It's taking what we've been doing to a new level."

She looked up at me then began unbuttoning her shirt. "Will you shut up already? Less talk, more dick."

I tossed the handcuffs on the bed, set the key on the bedside table where it would be easy to reach… just in case. I stripped off my utility belt then the rest of my clothes as I watched Charlie do the same.

When she was completely bare to me, I circled around her, took in every ebony inch of her. Fucking stunning.

I grabbed the cuffs and clipped them onto one wrist, left the other side dangling.

"Crawl up the bed. Show me that gorgeous ass on the way."

She did as told, and I had to take my dick in hand as I watched her on hands and knees, her ass and pussy on perfect view for me before she dropped onto her back.

I stalked after her, coming over her and taking her cuffed wrist and lifting it over her head. I took the other and brought it up beside it, but caught the chain around the slat of the headboard then clicked the cuff around her other wrist.

Her head was tilted back as she looked up at what I'd done. Then she tugged, testing the restraint. She wasn't going anywhere. As a shifter, I could break the slat on the headboard with a swift tug with my hand, but she didn't know that.

"Okay?" I asked, looking in her eyes for reaction as much as her words.

She nodded, licked her lips, then gave me the verbal "Yes" I wanted.

"Good girl." I kissed her on the lips, but didn't linger. I had so much more of her body to get my mouth on. Her nipples drew my eye, and I visited one, then the other, warming her up slowly.

We'd been wild and frantic for each other. This time, I was going to take my time. Savor. Even if my wolf and my dick were in disagreement.

"Did you know I was a tit guy?" I asked, taking a turgid tip into my mouth.

"Levi," she breathed. "You're going to drive me crazy, aren't you?"

I glanced up at her from the valley between her breasts. Grinned. "That's the plan."

I had to hope Clint or Rob would clear everyone out of the downstairs because things were going to get loud. Loud enough where Rob, Willow and Colton would probably hear Charlie from the main house. Too bad. I'd heard them all often enough.

Charlie groaned.

I kissed my way down to her navel, then lower and lower still, using my hands to spread her thighs wide, so I could settle between. "I like your tits, doll, but I *love* your pussy."

And I showed her how much.

———

CHARLIE

"Levi," I cried again. The guy was ruthless with his tongue. I wasn't going to survive this. Every ion in my being was focused on the tip of his tongue and how it flicked over my clit. Was he following the alphabet? A compass? I couldn't tell north from south, A from G. All I knew was that I liked that swirl, and I liked it *right there.*

"Levi!" I screamed when he pushed me over with one little flick of his wicked tongue.

My knees were clamped around his ears, and my body was tense from the pleasure. I was hot all over, my skin coated in sweat. And all he'd done was put his mouth on me. He hadn't even touched me with anything else yet.

He pushed himself up on his hands. I blinked, watching his talented tongue as he licked his lips. I wanted to touch him, to put my fingers in his hair and tug him down for a kiss. But all I got when I moved my wrists was restraint. I couldn't do anything.

Levi had me completely at his mercy.

"That was one."

"One?" I asked, my voice breathless.

"You don't think I'm done yet, do you?"

I shook my head.

His hand cupped my pussy, and I hissed, my clit sensitive. I was wet, and he stroked over me, spreading my wetness, then sliding his fingers into me. I writhed and moaned as he worked me but was thankful when he set his hand by my head, so he loomed over then kissed me.

I tasted myself on his tongue, but I wanted the kiss. Needed it. I was going to come again, and I couldn't stop it. After his exploring on other times we'd had sex, he'd found my g-spot and honed in on it now. It was like a turbo button for my arousal. Stroking it with his fingers pushed me to come faster and more intensely than I ever imagined.

When I came this time, there was no sound, but it was powerful nonetheless.

"Levi, please."

"Ah, begging. I love it."

The fucker.

But I felt his dick, hard and thick against my thigh, knew that he wanted in me as much as I wanted him to be there. He was holding off. Waiting. Dare I say he was playing with me? But he wasn't doing it as a taunt. No. He was doing it because he liked giving me pleasure. The handcuffs ensured he could do that without me distracting him or changing his mind. I was trying to now with the begging.

He reached for the side table and the thinning stash of condoms. I watched as he slid one down the thick length of him, readying himself.

With a hand on my hip, he rolled me over slowly, careful to make sure my wrists were fine in the cuffs as I settled on my stomach. Then he helped me to my knees, ass up, head down.

With my arms stretched taut over my head and my breasts pressed into the mattress, there was only one place he could play. My pussy.

I gasped though, when his hand came down in a gentle swat. His palm cupped the sting away. It was when his finger slipped between the seam of my ass to touch my back entrance did I startle. I'd been wrong. Naive. There was more than one place he could play. And I was still a virgin there.

"Shh," he crooned, his thumb brushing over me there with the lightest of caresses. "I'm not taking you here... tonight."

When his hand moved away, I relaxed back into the bed, but realized it had felt good to be touched... *there*. I never knew. I knew people did it, but I'd never thought I'd be one to like it.

Why should I be surprised though? Everything Levi did

with me I liked. I trusted him with my body. Hell, I was handcuffed to the bed and—

"Ah!" I hissed as he slipped into me in one long, smooth stroke. Bottoming out, his thighs pressed against mine.

His hand slid down my spine in a soothing caress.

"I can't get enough of you," he admitted. "Each time, it's like the first. It's never enough."

His strokes became harder. Impossibly deeper.

All I could do was hang on.

His hands gripped my hips, held me in place.

"Levi!" I cried, needing more.

Somehow he knew what that meant because I didn't. He was fucking me hard. Fast, his hips like a piston. How could I need more?

His hand slipped around beneath me and circled where we were joined, then used that wetness to coat my clit, to circle it lightly with his fingers. Then pinch it.

I came, tossing my head back. The groan that tore from me was almost primitive, the pleasure so intense. Colors danced behind my eyelids, and I rode it out. Levi didn't stop his rough taking of me, but I felt his rhythm change. He was losing control.

Once, twice and he literally growled as he came in me, buried deep.

A kiss landed on my sweaty shoulder. A lick. Even a little nip with his teeth.

When he pulled out, I slumped onto the bed. Done for.

I felt him return and release my wrists from the cuffs. He pulled me into his arms, snuggled me against him, and I slept. Safe. My mind only thinking of the arms that held me. That my own bed was too far away across the hall.

That I was right where I wanted to be.

 HARLIE

I WAS thankful Levi was in the shower when my cell rang. Bob, the lead foreman at Claymore's, called. I was in the bunkhouse kitchen making coffee, the phone wedged between my ear and my shoulder. The sun was just popping up over the eastern plains, and it was just so dang lovely. It was early for a work chat, but when working with animals, everyone started early.

"She seems to be doing well. So far, so good," I told him when he asked about Seraphina. I was to meet Clint at the stable in a little while for another go with Eddison. The horses were familiar with each other now, and it made the breeding process go a little more smoothly. Although, a stirred up stallion should never be underestimated.

"Well, I'm glad. I know everyone around here will be eager for a new foal," he replied. "I was calling because a package from the online vet pharmacy came in the other day. I'm sorry I forgot to call you sooner."

"Right, yes. No worries. You forgot to tell me, and I forgot that it was coming," I said, trying to remain calm and sound... normal.

"Well, I opened it up to make sure none of it needed to be refrigerated."

I bit my lip, trying not to gasp. He'd opened the shipment. Shit!

He'd done the right thing. I would have done it, too. There was nothing worse than learning medicine or vitamins spoiled because they hadn't been put into the stable's fridge.

"That's a lot of ketamine," he commented, adding a whistle to the end.

Play it cool. Play it cool.

"Oh? The order was for about ten thousand milligrams, if I remember correctly." I came up with a number I'd ordered *before* Dax started fucking with me.

"Well, I'd say this is more like a hundred thousand."

"That much?" I replied. Taking a deep breath, I lied through my teeth. "It sounds like they got the order wrong. That's more ketamine than we need or that I wanted. If they overshipped, I'll have to let them know although... I guess we'll go through it eventually. As long as it doesn't expire, it should still be good."

He gave a small laugh. "Maybe you hit one too many zeros with your keyboard in the order. My wife placed an order through the grocery store pickup. You know what I'm talking about, right? It pretty much saved our marriage."

Bob was a talker, which was sometimes frustrating when I had things to do, but today I was pleased. It meant he'd moved on from the drug delivery.

"Well, she wanted one package of coffee filters but somehow hit ten. That extra zero means we'll never need to buy them again in our lifetime."

"I think you're right. I know who to come to if I run out," I replied mildly. "Filters, not ketamine."

He laughed. "Right. I'll let you get back to it. Don't worry none about the package or anything else. I locked it in your office until you get back."

After I tucked my phone in my pocket and took my first sip of coffee, I leaned against the counter and wondered what I was going to do.

Bob knew about the order. Knew it was ketamine, and we'd received a large quantity. How was I going to just give it to Dax? I couldn't dose all the horses in Claymore's stables with that much of the drug to justify its disappearance. It wasn't like I could *lose* that many vials. That would be unprofessional and raise more red flags.

I was in over my head. I should've gone to the police to begin with. Handed over Dax and let him get fired and take the heat. I'd been so, so stupid!

I had to do the right thing. I had to take the shipment to the police. Tell Mr. Claymore the truth. How?

My cell beeped, and I pulled it out, read the text from Keely.

I didn't see the words because the answer came to me right then and there. The texts. Holy shit, I had the texts from Dax. The ones that said he wanted me to get the ketamine, asking where it was, threatening me. I could go to the police and show them the proof. There would be consequences for the product information I'd given to him before, but I'd face them. Yeah, it was time to deal. The stress was going to finish me otherwise.

LEVI

"LEVI, THIS IS INCREDIBLE!" Charlie gasped. Instead of a hike, we'd gone on horseback to the Sheffield property, on the ridge above a swimming hole formed by a waterfall and hot spring mixed together. The owner had inherited the place over a year ago and had yet to move in. I'd been friendly with Old Man Sheffield, and even though he'd been gone a while, I missed him still.

I'd been itching to take her here ever since I heard she went horseback riding with Clint and Johnny, and I nearly punched all their teeth out. I was the one who was to show her around, not them.

"Is this part of Rob's ranch?"

"No, but we have permission to use it. The owner's out of state right now, and we look after her property."

I swung off my mare and tethered her to a tree. Charlie started to dismount Seraphina, and I caught her around the waist as she descended.

"Oh."

I didn't mind showing off my shifter strength as I held her suspended in the air for a moment before gently lowering her to her feet. I loved the way it felt to hold her entire weight in my hands, her widened eyes locked on mine. My wolf was content knowing she was in my hold, that she was safe, protected. Mine.

"Oh," I repeated and brushed my lips across hers. What I felt for her wasn't passionate or wild. It was different. Oh, I wanted to fuck her hard and thoroughly, but I wanted to cherish her, too. I grabbed a blanket I'd tied in a roll on the back of my mare.

"Is this the romantic spot where you take all your conquests?" she asked, glancing about.

I could tell she was trying for light, but I heard the rasp of jealousy behind the words. The same jealousy I'd felt when she went riding with the other guys. Good.

"Never," I swore immediately, to put her mind at rest. "This is sort of a secret spot for us on Wolf Ranch. I know Boyd took Audrey here when they were dating."

That had been a cluster, the asshole Markle shooting a shifter kid in front of them. Thank fuck, the kid was fine after all that *and* that Audrey was cool with discovering her mate was a shifter.

I tucked her hand in mine and led her down the incline. "You're the first and only woman I've brought here." That was the truth. Shifters didn't get involved with humans— not even half-breeds who couldn't shift, like me. We didn't date females and bring them onto or near the ranch. At least until recently. In fact, until the latest spate of matings to humans, no one in our pack ever invited a human around.

Ever. It was a wonder the guys had ever found their mates.

"Come on," she pressed, nudging me, clearly not believing my words.

"It's the truth. I am not a ladies' man. You were the first woman to spend the night in my bed."

Confusion flitted over her face. "That—can't be... "

"What's puzzling you?"

"Well, I know I'm inexperienced, but you sure seemed to know what you were doing. I thought I had been the virgin."

I laughed. "I've practiced a bit, yeah. One night stands and crap like that." I wasn't going to go into any more detail than that. None of the previous women mattered. I meant what I said. They'd only been practice for her. "Not a beautiful woman spending the night in my bed."

Charlie's expression went soft and open, like it did when she was tending to animals. It made my chest tight because she was giving *me* that look.

Shit. I was falling for her.

The thought startled me. This wasn't how I'd thought my life would go. I'd hoped to mate a shifter and have kids who could actually shift and not be stuck with a wolf inside who was incapable of being free. But with Charlie... none of that seemed to matter. I forgot about the pain of my predicament. Of what had happened in the past. I just cared about her. The now.

Spending time with her.

Getting her off.

Making her scream.

Hell, making her happy.

The watering hole was tucked in at the side of the mountain, a steep cliff looming on one side where there was a waterfall that filled the deep pool. It was also heated from beneath by a thermal hot spring, making the water warm all year round.

We stopped on the bank, and I tossed my hat down on the ground and started stripping out of my clothes. Charlie's mouth opened in surprise. "Are we going... skinny dipping?"

I grinned, not the least bit shamed about being naked outside. While I didn't shift and run like the others, I wasn't modest. "We sure are. Don't worry, the water's warm."

"It is?" She crouched by the water's edge and swirled her fingertips in the clear water. "Oh wow. It's perfect." She flushed a little, looking around first, as if we might have observers, then shucked her clothing and waded in.

I stood and watched the little strip show, my dick getting hard.

I ran up behind and slapped her ass, catching her around the waist and lifting her to carry as I waded into the deep part. I wanted her with me, feeling her body all wet and warm in the water.

"Mmm, this is perfect," she murmured, relaxing and letting her hands float on the surface.

I turned her around to face me, and her legs wrapped around my back. My hard dick nestled into the seam of her pussy.

"It's been nice having you here this week," I said, trying to keep my thoughts off of my dick and the fact that if I just shifted her a little bit, I'd be buried deep inside her.

"It's been amazing," she agreed, looping her arms around my neck. "I don't just mean the sex."

The thought of her leaving next week already made me want to tear down a tree.

"How attached are you to that job of yours in Colorado?"

Whoa. Had that fallen out of my mouth?

I hadn't meant to inquire. I really wasn't even sure what I was suggesting. It just came out. Yet I wanted to know the answer.

Her expression turned wistful. "Pretty attached. It pays well, and if I end up needing to get someone in to care for Pops during the day, that could get expensive. If I'm being realistic, that's going to happen and soon."

"Right, your Pops." I swallowed. I tried to never think of my grandparents. When I did, it was never in a caring or loving way. It was odd to take a blood relative into account since I had none. My brain ran through possibilities. Possibilities that involved Charlie and her grandfather moving out to Wolf Ranch. Cooper Valley could use another large animal veterinarian, and I was sure Audrey would have connections to support for memory care.

"Well, he'd be pretty safe out on a ranch," I found myself offering.

Charlie swallowed, locking gazes with me. "Wh-what are you saying?"

I shrugged. What *was* I saying? Did I really want to settle down and make a life with a human? It would mean our children surely wouldn't shift.

Our children?

Holy shit!

Was I really this far with my fantasies of not giving up Charlie?

Apparently I was. But shifters bonded more quickly than humans. She needed more than a week before she figured I might be more than just a fling.

We'd known each other for a week. A week! Most humans had leftovers in their fridge longer than that.

I didn't want to scare her off. So I hedged. "I'm just saying I like this." I gave her a squeeze. "I like *you*, Charlie." The words in my head were actually, *I love you*, but I didn't want to freak her out. She thought too much as it was. I didn't need to give her more to stew on.

"It's probably way too soon to start suggesting long-term things, but I also *don't* like the idea of you packing up next week and leaving forever. I'd really love to explore the possibility of something more."

Charlie's eyes misted, and she blinked rapidly. "Wow. Um. I don't know what to say."

Shut down. Totally. I had to pull back, recover, even though my words had been laid as bare as we were.

"Well, let's stay open to more," I hedged. "I mean, if you feel the same."

"I do," she said.

"Or we can just work on that orgasm chart I know is in your head. I'm guessing you need a few more for your tally."

She laughed. "Orgasm chart?"

"Not that? Well, since you were a virgin and all, I'm guessing you haven't had sex outdoors before?"

Her rolled eyes were the answer I was looking for.

"Give me an hour. You can cross that off your list."

I carried her out of the water, suddenly desperate to punch another hole in her sex bingo card—the one for outdoor sex. I laid her on the thick blanket I'd brought and showed her exactly how much fun it could be. I just had to stay focused on the fling... not the forever.

HARLIE

THE NEXT DAY, Levi had gone into town for a shift. He'd said goodbye as I'd been drinking my coffee in the bunkhouse kitchen. It was such a simple thing, but it showed that we were together. Sharing a living space. Sharing a bed. Sharing an intimate moment where a couple said goodbye to each other as we parted ways to spend our day at work.

It had been nice but scary, after what Levi had shared at the watering hole the day before. He'd admitted to wanting more. Even asked if I'd be interested in moving here. That... hell, that Audrey could help find care for Pops.

He'd been talking about things besides which position to fuck me in. He'd been talking about serious stuff. Real life stuff. Just like the morning goodbye kiss.

I'd been surprised. Stunned. Perhaps that was why I'd been so cautious in my answers. I hadn't expected him to want more although he hadn't given me any indication he'd been ready to stop. But he hadn't given any indication he'd been so... serious before either.

This kiss though. I kept going back to that simple kiss all day.

It had meant more to me than anything we'd done before. More than the playful sex. More than being tied up and giving him my trust. More than finding a stray dog on the side of the road.

It had meant things were... possible.

That I was wanted for *more.*

That had left me in a haze of thought, but thankfully, I was always that way it seemed because neither Clint or Johnny commented all day.

It made me think I could get past my messed up life. I wanted to ignore Dax. Everything about him. I knew how to get myself out of the mess, but I had to be in Colorado to do it. I had to get the shipment of ketamine from my office and take it to the police along with the texts from Dax. I had to share them with Mr. Claymore. Face the consequences.

But I couldn't avoid Dax. Or his calls. Fuck. I wanted to take my phone and flush it down the toilet. Hell, shove it into the manure pile on the far side of the stable. I just wanted it over. But Dax didn't know that, and I had to suck it up. Had to hold on for a little while longer.

"H-hello?"

"I'm sitting here having some dinner with a new friend," he said. His voice was surprisingly... light.

"Hi, sweetpea." I sucked in a sharp breath at hearing Pops on the other end, my heart flying to my throat. "A friend of yours stopped by to eat. Unlike you, he likes gravy on his dinner. Even on his green beans and pot roast."

My hands turned ice cold. I wanted to puke and faint at the same time.

Dax was *with* Pops. *In our house.*

I stood, paced. He knew where we lived. Had probably just knocked on the door, and Pops had let him in. Everyone liked Dax. Hell, everyone *fell* for his acting. Even my grandfather.

"Are you okay?" I asked, trying to sound calm.

He didn't sound upset or hurt. "Fine, sweetpea. We're going to watch some shows. Says he's going to stay with me while you're gone. Isn't that nice?"

Pops wouldn't have let a stranger stay in the house if he had all his faculties. This was a weak moment for him, and Dax was taking advantage.

"Can I talk to Dax again?" I asked, not wanting Pops to hand the phone off, wanting to keep talking to him, so I knew he was all right.

"Yeah?" Dax asked.

"You hurt him in any way, I'll—"

"You'll what? All I want is the package, *sweetpea.* Now."

"I'm in Montana," I countered.

"You have until tomorrow morning."

I stalled in my pacing. *Tomorrow morning?* "I can't get there by then!"

"Yes, you can. Move it, sweetheart. We'll be waiting."

He hung up.

I stared at my cell. None of that conversation had been recorded. It wasn't a text, so there was no proof of what he said. Of how he'd threatened me. The fact that Dax was in my house.

I had to go. I had to do as he said. My intentions to tell the police would have to wait. I had to give Dax what he wanted because he was *with* Pops. Adrenaline pumped through my veins. I couldn't stand still. Couldn't think straight. I had to go.

I had to go *now*. I had to get to my grandfather.

Shit. Seraphina.

Holy shit. *Levi*. Thankfully, he'd texted earlier and said he had to work a traffic accident and would be late, deciding to spend the night at Clint's parents' house in town. I wasn't thankful about the traffic accident, God. At least he wouldn't be here to stop me because I wasn't sure if I could leave if he did.

My heart literally broke in two with the idea of leaving him. Leaving without explanation, without saying goodbye. He wanted me to stay, and yet here I was, fleeing after dark without saying goodbye.

There was no alternative. It was better this way. He wanted me, the me he knew, not the me I'd been hiding. He couldn't know what I'd become. It was better to just leave, to have him think I bailed.

I couldn't lie to him. Not any more than I already had. If I had to look him in the eye now, I doubted I'd be able to come up with something that would justify an abrupt and hasty late-night departure.

Once he knew the truth, it would be over anyway. I had been prepared to face the consequences with the cops. With Mr. Claymore. But with Levi?

That cut sliced the deepest.

But I had to get to Pops. He was what mattered.

Fuck. Levi mattered. Too much. That was the problem here. If Levi was just a fling as we'd planned, I wouldn't have cared. He wouldn't have either to find me gone. But he was more. So much more.

I grabbed my bag, shoved all my things into it and ran for the stable. It took an hour to connect the trailer to the truck and get Seraphina settled within. Thankfully, Clint and Johnny were long gone for the night, and no one had come out of the main house.

Another few minutes, and I was on the road.

I was thankful it was late. No one could see me leaving. No one had stopped me. No one would know until morning. By then, I'd be back in Colorado, and Pops would be safe.

And Dax? I had a ten-hour drive to figure out what I was going to do with him. I just had to pry my thoughts away from Levi, who was getting further away with every dark, deserted mile that passed.

Levi, who had changed everything for me. It had been so much more than what I'd told Keely I'd do. He was more than a dick to punch my V-card. I'd learned to trust with him. To let go and enjoy my body. To enjoy another's body. To give and receive. To share.

To love.

After last night and what Levi had suggested, I'd had my own crazy thoughts—about staying in Montana. Or continuing some kind of long-distance relationship.

But I'd known it was crazy.

And Levi would never, ever continue a relationship with me once he learned what I'd done. What I was still doing. The mess I'd made of my life.

No, I had no choice but to leave him behind. I sniffed and wiped a tear running down my face with the back of my hand.

At least the memories would be intact.

EVI

"ROUGH NIGHT?"

I spun on my heel to see Clint and Willow walking my way from the stable. Clint carried a box under his arm.

I ran my hand over my face, yanked off my hat. "Jackknifed semi on the interstate. No one was hurt, but it was a clusterfuck."

I'd crashed hard at Janet and Tom's place in town. Things had finally been cleared, and I'd gotten to bed after two, yet I still woke with the sun. I'd tossed and turned all night, perhaps because I'd gotten used to having Charlie in my bed. Waking up without her hadn't been fun and something I wasn't looking forward to doing again.

"Well, there's somewhat of a cluster here, too," he said. Willow nodded.

I frowned. Everything seemed quiet and peaceful,

nothing like the wild scene on the highway. I liked early mornings on the ranch. Everything was quiet, calm. Fresh, as if the day was full of possibilities.

Clint came close enough to hand me the box. It was a typical shipping package, the top slit open. I peeked inside, nudged the filler aside. "Looks like vials of medicine. What's the issue?"

He tipped his chin toward the delivery. "That's ketamine. Used for horse tranquilizing. No big deal, especially around here."

"But I'm sure you know, on the streets, it's used for everything from mild sedative to a downer to date rape drug," Willow said.

The fucking things I learned as sheriff. "Yeah." I didn't like where this was going.

Clint nodded. "A vet might carry these. But two, maybe three vials."

I stuck my hand in the box, moved around the bubble wrap some more. "There's got to be fifty vials or more."

"Exactly."

I sighed, tired as hell and ready for some coffee. And Charlie time. I didn't know what the big deal was or why he was telling me about it. "So send some of it back."

"We didn't order it. It's a controlled substance. Only a veterinarian can order it."

I pursed my lips, trying not to yell at him for getting on with what exactly the cluster fuck was. "I'm fucking tired. Spill it, will you?"

"The package is addressed to Charlie," Willow said.

I flipped one side of the lid closed, saw her name and care of Wolf Ranch. Snippets of conversation I'd overheard of hers on the phone yesterday filtered back to me. I'd had no idea who she'd been talking to. It was one thing to overhear her chatting with someone about her sex life and how she'd wanted me involved in it. Another to snoop on a work call, which it clearly had been. But I'd heard the word *ketamine.*

But no. I couldn't believe Charlie would be mishandling drugs. She was so responsible. Fastidious. I was sure she even had a document that listed every purchase.

"Clint came to get me when he saw this package," Willow said with a mournful expression. "I'm sorry, Levi, but something's definitely not right here." She was former DEA. She would know. Still, I couldn't believe it.

"So let's ask her about it." I glanced to the bunkhouse, then thumbed over my shoulder. "If you missed her in the stable, maybe she's inside. I hope she made a big pot of coffee."

Willow shook her head. "She's not here."

"Fine, then when she gets back. I need to either get an IV of caffeine or hit the sack for a few more hours." I turned toward the bunkhouse and my bed, wishing Charlie wasn't in town or off with the other women or whatever she was doing, so she could get under the covers with me.

"She's gone."

I froze, turned around, set my hands on my hips.

"Say what?"

"Gone."

"*Gone,*" I repeated, my world going up in smoke.

"Her stuff's gone. Truck's gone. Trailer's gone. Seraphina's gone."

"Gone? You've gotta be fucking with me. I texted with her last night around eight." The words fell out over stiff lips. Clint didn't play around like Johnny did. Not about something like this. He knew I'd throat punch him.

He shrugged, ran a hand over his neck, his tell that he

was frustrated. "She's gone. Snuck out. I only figured it out when I couldn't find Seraphina. I first thought maybe she'd taken her for a ride or something. It's a pretty morning, and she'd enjoyed it when Johnny and I had showed her around. But no."

"Gone?" I said once more. *What the fuck?*

He held up a hand. "Look, I know you two were close."

Were? How about *are.* I stared at him. He knew *close* was a diplomatic word for *fucking.*

He pointed to the box I'd forgotten I was even holding. "That order... the itemized list tucked inside matches the quantity. She ordered a shit ton of Vitamin K."

"It's Vitamin K on the streets. You're using the slang term as if that's what she does—peddles the shit."

He arched a brow. "What do you know of her?"

"What do I know?" I knew she was a workaholic. She was close with her grandfather. I knew she had sensitive nipples. I knew she was ticklish on the backside of her knees. I knew she had a little mole on the inside of her right thigh I liked to kiss before I got to her pussy. It was like the north star leading me home.

He pointed at the box. "This was delivered for her, and now she's gone. Disappeared, gone."

"You think something happened to her?" I freaked a little at the possibility. I glanced around as if she might be in a ditch nearby needing me to save her.

"She took everything," he told me. "If she was injured or something happened with Seraphina, she would have told us that shit. No one sneaks off in the middle of the night because things are okay. Something's up with her, and I think it has to do with that." He pointed at the box.

"She's not a drug dealer." Now I was pissed at their accusations, but the box didn't lie. What did she want to do with this much ketamine? Why have it shipped here? Seraphina didn't need all that shit, and if she did need some, we could get it from the vet in town.

Why the secret? Why sneak away?

I pulled out my phone, texted her.

Me: Where are you, doll?

I waited thirty seconds. A minute. Nothing.

"I called Claymore to see if they showed up," he told me. "Nothing. He seemed surprised she'd even left, which means her trip hadn't been planned or expected."

"It's a long fucking drive," I said. "Maybe she's just not there yet." I couldn't imagine her driving through the night. While the roads were fairly flat between here and Colorado, there was a shit ton of wildlife. I knew the stats about cars vs. animals all too well.

"Look, I know you guys had a fling, but she's got you by the balls. She's into some shit, and you need to let her go. That box is bad news."

I shoved it into his chest—which was tamer than what I wanted to do to him—and walked into the bunkhouse, slammed the door shut. Taking the stairs two at a time, I pushed open her bedroom door. It was empty. I stalked across the hall to my room. She was neat as a fucking pin, but I thought maybe she'd left a thing or two on the floor. Nothing. The bathroom was picked clean of anything feminine. Not even a pink razor in the shower.

Clint was right. She was gone. I stalked down the stairs.

I paced, kicked a chair, tossed my hat onto the couch.

Why the fuck did she leave? Why wasn't she answering my text? I immediately went to the worst, that she was in a ditch somewhere and couldn't respond, but no. She'd intentionally left. And done so while I wasn't here. That thought alone was like a strike below the belt. She'd known

I would be in town. I'd texted her and told her. Was that why she left so she wouldn't have to face me?

And the ketamine? I tried to remember what I'd overheard yesterday morning.

That's more ketamine than we need or that I wanted... As long as it doesn't expire, it should still be good.

Goddammit. Now that I reviewed that conversation, it sounded like she'd ordered ketamine to be delivered in Colorado, too. *What the fuck?* Who the hell had she been talking to?

And then there was the way she'd gone quiet after I talked to the aspiring drug dealer at the fair. The questions she asked about what sentence he'd face.

Sometimes people get themselves into things without fully understanding the consequences.

I picked up the chair I'd kicked and smashed it against the wall. It splintered into all kinds of satisfying pieces.

"Whoa," Rob said as he came in, his voice low, hands out in front of him. Like I was a horse that needed calming.

I whirled and glared at him. My vision had strangely narrowed and sharpened. My focus was razor sharp. My hearing honed in on his heartbeat.

Rob flicked his brows. "Heard Charlie left," he said mildly.

My stomach tumbled like towels in a dryer. My brain did the same thing.

I gave the wall a thud with the soft part of my fist although punching a hole through it would be more satisfying. "Did you hear about the ketamine?"

He nodded.

I wasn't sure if Clint and Willow were tattletales or saviors because I didn't feel like explaining the horse tranquilizer shit to Rob. I didn't even understand it myself.

"Sounds like she got herself in trouble," he commented. While I took it as an accusation, he was only stating fact.

"Charlie's not a fucking drug dealer," I snarled, too defensively. But she couldn't be. I was sure of it. She was too good for that. I *knew* her. Didn't I?

"No, but a drug dealer needs a supplier."

I clenched my hands into fists. "You met her. We all did. Hell, have you ever met anyone else who has ironed jeans? Or wears makeup and jewelry to breed a horse? Tell me why the fuck she would be anyone's fucking supplier."

Shaking his head, he dropped his hands to his hips. Sighed. "People do it for different reasons."

I thought about her grandfather. What she'd said about needing to keep her well-paying job to afford a caretaker for him. But she still wouldn't sell drugs to see that happen. No way.

I was so angry I saw red. I saw every ridge of the plaster on the far wall. My wolf snarled, ready to go after Rob. He didn't like a word Rob was insinuating, even if Clint had started it.

He tipped his chin. "Want to take that gun off your hip?"

I narrowed my eyes. "Why? Are you going to tell me something else that will want to make me shoot you?"

He scoffed lightly. "Like that would kill me."

Only because he was my alpha and his command held a physical compulsion, I unhooked my utility belt and dropped it on the back of the couch. They'd been put back in place when Willow and Marina insisted Shadow and the puppies be moved to the laundry room at the main house.

"Here's what we do know," he told me. "She had a big order of ketamine delivered here. A place where it could go unnoticed. Now she's gone. Left before the breeding was done."

"Yeah, I got all that," I snapped, not eager to listen to a thing he said.

I took a step toward him, slapped my hand down on the counter. "You're so fucking calm. Don't you care?"

"Do you?" he asked.

"Stop being such a fucking asshole."

He gave a slight shrug. "She was a fling, you said. Two weeks. Why should it bother you if she's mixed up in something with ketamine. She did you a favor leaving as she did. She's a drug pusher. You're the county sheriff. This way you don't even have to say goodbye. Or arrest her."

I narrowed my eyes at him. He was pissing me off. My wolf stood up and howled.

"No hooks to pull out and escape from," he added.

My wolf snapped.

"Don't speak of her that way," I snarled.

I leaned forward a little, ready to stalk over to him and wipe that calm look off his face.

"Why not?" He shrugged, as if he was talking about the weather, not Charlie. "So you had a little fun. She's got secrets. Big ones. She's not your mate."

Yeah, we had fun. I thought of how she'd laughed when I'd tossed her over my shoulder and carried her upstairs. The way she'd looked up at me from beneath her sooty lashes as she sucked my dick down into her throat. How she'd looked handcuffed to my bed, my hands holding onto her lush hips. The kindness she showed with Shadow. The way she stroked Seraphina.

"She's mine," I snarled, breathing hard.

He shook his head. "She's not your mate. She's gone. Back to Colorado. You were a quick fuck to her."

And that was it. Those were the words that pushed me over the edge.

I lunged toward Rob, and the next thing I knew I felt pain in my muscles, my bones. Things shifted and moved. The sound of ripping cloth, cracking joints filled the air.

One second, I was ready to punch Rob in the jaw, the next I was running toward him on four paws.

My vision sharpened, my hearing honed. I smelled. Holy fuck, did I scent. The lemony tang of floor cleaner. The scent of the dogs. Rob's deodorant or soap. And Charlie. I smelled her on the air.

I knew her cinnamon scent, but this was more. Heightened. I launched myself at Rob but he knocked me away. "*Sit down.*" I'd never felt alpha command before. Not really. Not like I did right then. It reverberated into every cell, as if his voice could control every organ in my body. I instantly skidded around and sat down on my haunches and breathed deep. As a fucking wolf.

I'd shifted. Holy fuck. And I scented Charlie.

My mate.

I glanced up at Rob. Yeah, up because I was only a few feet tall.

"I thought so," he said, the corner of his mouth tipped up.

I growled.

He grinned, then squatted down in front of me.

"Charlie's your mate, huh?"

I lifted my nose to the sky and howled.

He laughed. The fucker laughed. "Before you bite my throat out, let's get you to shift back. Then we'll figure out what's going on with her. How to get her back."

I stilled, realized I had no fucking idea how to shift back. I'd never been in wolf form before. I'd seen others do it hundreds... thousands of times. But me?

Fuck, I was a wolf! And Charlie—my... *human* mate...

had brought it out. With a little help from Rob and his intentional word jabs.

"Stay calm. It's fine."

I snapped at him again. I was thirty-three years old, and I'd never done this before. Hell, I felt like Charlie, a virgin in my own right.

Rob narrowed his eyes, took a deep breath. "*Shift,*" he said, his voice booming, the deep alpha tone rippling through me. I wanted to roll over and show him my belly. Lift my neck, showing him I meant no disrespect. But my wolf obeyed instinctively, and somehow, I shifted back. I had no control in the action, which was probably a good thing.

I was on the floor, fucking naked, my clothes in torn tatters around me. I ran my hand over my face, looked at Rob. "I fucking hate you."

He stood, grinned again as he grabbed a throw blanket from the back of a couch and tossed it at me. "Yeah, well, being alpha's a bitch. Now let's figure out what to do about your mate."

HARLIE

THE STUFFED wolf Levi won for me at the county fair rode shotgun with me the whole way back to Colorado. I'd even buckled the stupid thing in like it was real.

I was losing my mind.

By the time I got back, I'd driven through the night, fueled by strong truck stop coffee and my gnawing anxiety. Ten hours was a long time when there was nothing to do but stay on the highway and make sure no animals ran under my tires. The techno beat of my workout playlist had helped keep me awake, but it didn't stop my mind from wandering.

Every mile I drove the ache in my chest grew stronger.

Leaving Levi felt like the biggest mistake of my life.

I'd really love to explore the possibility of something more. We'd been in the most glorious spot, looking back the most romantic, too. He'd looked into my eyes and suggested I move with Pops to Montana. To be with him.

And yeah, that was crazy considering we'd only known each other for a week, but it also felt so right. I cared about Levi. I cared about more than just his prowess in bed. He was honest and good. Courageous and strong. He'd taken a job as sheriff because he believed in justice.

And Wolf Ranch? I loved it there. The place... called to me, just like Levi did. It was the land, the laid back friendliness of everyone. The family feeling.

Levi hadn't wanted me to move there because he felt the ranch needed a vet. No, he'd wanted me. Accepted that I came with an ailing grandfather. He wanted me as part of the family.

Hell, a family with him, however that was shaped.

It felt like I'd just run away from my future. A future I hadn't known I'd wanted, but now that I shut the door on it felt more tragic than anything I'd been through. Well, other than having Dax call from inside my house. But that wasn't tragic, that was terror-inducing.

But I had to remember that even if Dax hadn't called, even if I hadn't had to leave and drive through the night, my past would've caught up to me.

I was glad I wasn't going to be around when Levi found out who I really was. The mess I'd gotten myself into. I was a coward and couldn't imagine seeing his face. I remembered how he'd been with that teenager at the fair. He'd been young and stupid. I wasn't young, but I was feeling pretty stupid. If he'd wanted that kid to spend the night in jail to learn his lesson, I could only imagine what he'd want as a consequence for someone like me. It wasn't going to be handcuffs in his bed.

Under normal circumstances, I would've driven straight to Mr. Claymore's ranch to drop off Seraphina, but these weren't normal circumstances. My grandfather was in danger and had been since Dax had called. Instead, I drove straight to the house where I could negotiate with Dax. Get him away from Pops and tell him I'd get him the ketamine locked in my office at Mr. Claymore's.

So I drove into my neighborhood at eight in the morning still hauling the horse trailer behind the ranch truck. I had to park it in the street since there was no way I could back it out of the driveway later.

Stomach gurgling and rancid from no food and only caffeine, I jumped out of the truck.

I dashed into the house, slipping on the rug in the entry with my haste. "Pops!" I called.

I heard his heavy footfall coming from the kitchen. "Well, look who's here," he said with a big grin. "Aren't you a sight for sore eyes. How's my girl?"

I looked around. Dax wasn't following him. Wasn't in the living room, behind the curtains. "Are you alone?" I asked instead of answering him.

He frowned, just noticing my panic. Taking a deep breath, I tried to calm down because he didn't seem upset. "Yes, but Mrs. Vasquez said she'd stop by later to go through the newspaper fliers with me. She likes to cut out the good coupons. I was just putting my breakfast dishes in the dishwasher then was going to change into a new shirt because I spilled a little jelly on this one." Patting his chest, I saw a red smear.

"Oh." I went past him down the hall to the kitchen. No, Dax wasn't hiding in the pantry.

"It's Sunday, and I don't want to miss the late service," he said, following behind. "I hope Mrs. Abrams brings those little barbecue drumettes for the lunch after. I love those."

Okay. Everything was fine. Too fine. I turned to face him, leaned against the peach colored counter. The kitchen hadn't been updated since I was in grade school. "On the phone last night, you had a visitor."

He nodded his gray haired head. "Nice fellow. Said he worked with you."

I bobbed my head in agreement and said, "That's right. How late did he stay?"

He put his finger to his lip, his usual thinking gesture. "Not past eight. I like my shows."

Dax had left at eight. Maybe fifteen minutes after he called me. Fuck. I wasn't sure if I wanted to cry or scream. He'd had me drive through the night thinking that Pops was in danger. Immediate danger. There was no question he knew where we lived and had easily gained Pops' trust. Dax wasn't any less of an issue than the night before, but what he'd said on the phone and reality didn't match.

I had never wanted to kill someone so much in my life. I'd driven all night! And shit, Seraphina was still in the trailer out front.

Since everything was fine and there was no real reason to have him cancel his usual plans for church and an afternoon spent with friends at a luncheon, I told him, "I stopped in on the way to the stable to say hi. I have to get the horse into a paddock to stretch her legs."

He came over to me, and gave me a hug. "It's good to have you home, sweetpea. I just didn't expect you until next week sometime."

Me neither.

"Want me to give you a ride to church on my way?"

He shook his head. "The Merrimans are picking me up."

"Right." That was the routine for Sunday mornings. He was picked up by fellow church members who lived a few streets over, stayed for the organized lunch after. I rarely went with him because I often worked.

At least he would be with others and out of the house if Dax decided to return.

I closed my eyes, took a breath. I wanted to go upstairs and climb into bed and sleep for about ten hours. But Seraphina needed to be let out of the trailer, and I had a blackmailing asshole to finish.

I couldn't wait any longer. I didn't *want* to. It was time to find Dax and finish him.

I just had to hope it didn't finish me in the process.

25

EVI

I HAD A MATE. I was a fully shifting wolf, and I'd found my mate.

Ordinarily it would be cause for celebration, but considering my mate was a goddamn drug dealer who'd left during the night without even saying goodbye, I wasn't feeling all that chipper.

In fact, it was all I could do not to rip the inside of the airplane to shreds.

Yeah, I was on a plane. Nothing worse than that for a prowling wolf than a tin can in the sky.

I hadn't thought what else to do. My wolf sure as shit wasn't going to sit at Wolf Ranch and stew over my mate walking out on us.

And I needed to know about this ketamine thing.

Like, how was it possible that the beautiful, kind,

responsible vet I knew and loved had become a drug supplier.

It didn't make sense.

I'd thought about it the entire plane ride, which was thankfully only about an hour.

I kept coming back to that one thing she'd said in the truck after the county fair.

Sometimes people get themselves into things without fully understanding the consequences.

It wasn't an excuse. Especially since Charlie was way too smart to not understand consequences. But she was innocent. Naive.

It was possible she'd gotten herself into some kind of predicament.

Maybe she even required help. That she was in over her head and needed me to save her. To protect her.

That thought had my wolf snarling. I felt him, right beneath the surface, struggling to get free. He wanted to protect Charlie.

But I didn't even know if she needed my protection. Or would want it. Her bailing in the middle of the night was a pretty sure indication she might not want anything to do with me. Then again, maybe she was protecting me?

My wolf didn't like that at all. Charlie was a fragile human. I was *really* hard to kill.

Fuck—what would I do if it turned out she was a drug supplier? That she wasn't who I'd believed she was? Would I be able to walk away from my mate, right when I'd found her? Would I be okay turning her in to the local police? How could I have a mate behind bars?

I probably wouldn't go moon mad as a half-breed. Thankfully, I wasn't that alpha. But still, I didn't know what it would do to my wolf. I might go a different flavor of insane. The human kind.

Fuck! I crushed the half-full water bottle in my hand just as the plane touched down, causing water to flood over my legs and the floor. The guy on the other side of the aisle gave me the side-eye, but I didn't give a fuck what people thought about me.

All I cared about was this shit with Charlie.

I got off the plane and marched to the rental car counter, where all they had was a tiny white compact two door.

"Fine," I growled, signing the damn papers, not giving a shit. I'd cram my body into a car three sizes smaller if it meant getting to my mate. As long as it had an engine and wheels, I didn't care if it was a clown car.

As I jammed my legs under the dash, I came around to the same thought I'd had the whole flight over: there had to be an explanation. The woman I knew wouldn't be in the drug trade for money. It just wasn't like her.

I couldn't believe it. I *wouldn't*.

I would show up and demand an explanation—for the ketamine and for leaving without a goodbye. And not accepting my calls or texts.

Then I would tell her I was a wolf.

That she was my mate.

After that, we'd figure shit out from there.

As far as plans went, it was pretty fucking flimsy, but it was the best I had.

Because everything—my life, my future, my sanity— revolved around that woman. I just had to pray to fate this was salvageable.

 HARLIE

CLAYMORE'S HORSE property was nothing like Wolf Ranch. Nestled in the foothills of the mountains above Denver, it sprawled in a large open expanse between the rugged terrain. There were acres to ride, but the mountains that surrounded it on all sides were unforgiving. This area was nothing like Montana. Claymore's house—mansion—was set back from the road but was visible to all who drove by. It appeared to be intentional. Claymore's wealth was on full display. The stable was state-of-the-art. The fencing around the corrals and paddocks was metal and indestructible. Everything was immaculately groomed and... perfect.

Just like I'd tried to be. A week at Wolf Ranch, with the neverending prairie and big sky, I felt almost claustrophobic as I pulled up behind the back side of the stable. There was a gate to the paddock there with room to park the trailer. I wanted to get Seraphina outside to stretch her legs not confined to a stall.

So much had happened while I was gone, which had only been about a week. I'd changed. I'd lost my virginity, but that was just a label. I'd opened up—and not just my legs—to Levi. Others, too. I saw that work wasn't everything, that being there for Pops was what was important. And other connections.

Levi.

Fuck. No, I wasn't going to think about him now.

Hopping from the truck, I went around to the back of the trailer to let Seraphina out.

"You!" Dax shouted, and I jumped a foot as the sound echoed around the inside of the metal trailer. Seraphina tossed her head and tried to retreat, even though she and Dax were buddies. Maybe, like me, she'd had a change of heart about him.

My heart leapt into my throat and adrenaline pumped through me as I grabbed her lead and tried to calm her. I didn't say anything until I led the horse out of the trailer.

"Don't spook a horse, you idiot!" I hissed.

"Where's the fucking K?" Dax didn't look like himself. The boyish good-looks disappeared, replaced with a menacing scowl. His hair was a mess, and his skin seemed sallow. Dark bags were under his eyes. Mine, probably too.

"In my office, I would assume," I countered, with a shit ton of sass. "I just got back. You know, from driving straight through the night because you were with my grandfather?"

A sly smile spread across his face. "It got your ass back here, didn't it?"

I didn't respond to that. Nothing I could say would make a difference. All I'd do is show how much he got to me, how much he was controlling me. Hell, I felt like a puppet. *His* puppet.

"So get me in the office."

"Seraphina's been in the trailer all night because you're a fucking asshole." I pulled the keys from my jeans pocket, tossed them at him. "I'm putting her in the paddock. You get in the office yourself."

I turned away, not waiting for him to respond. He had the keys if he wanted to get the drugs. As I opened the gate and led Seraphina through and into the tall grass, I heard him head toward the stable and no doubt my office within. I figured I had about a minute at most before he came back.

I pulled my cell from my pocket and with a racing heart and fumbling fingers, I found the photo setting, pulled up the video feature and hit record. I dashed to the trailer and set the phone down on the wheel well bump-out.

I grabbed a shovel that was affixed to the interior wall of the trailer used to scoop manure, but Dax came back out. "Where's the shipment you got in Montana?"

My heart pounded so hard I was sure he could hear it. I wasn't good at being tricky. Or sly. But I was smarter than him.

"The shipment of ketamine you made me order?" I asked, my voice clear and as calm as I could make it.

"Uh, yeah," he said in a *duh* voice. "That one."

"You called me last night from my own house, sitting with my grandfather. You threatened to harm him if I didn't get back here right away."

Dax narrowed his eyes. "So? Your gramps is fine. I didn't do shit to him except eat some dinner. Too much fucking gravy."

"So I left Montana last night a week early because of you. The shipment hadn't arrived before I left. And I can hardly request it now. Not without an explanation. You've got plenty in your hands from the shipment you made me get before I left. What are you going to do with it all?"

He hoisted up his pants. "Sell it. You're my supplier now, right, Charlie? I got you good."

"How's that?" I held onto the shovel handle, the tip of it in the ground.

"You're part of the supply chain. In fact, the police go harder on suppliers than they do on peddlers of drugs. So you're in this deep."

I shook my head, even though I was quaking in my boots. "No. I'm not in this at all. I only started it because you threatened me."

He took a step toward me, but I held my ground. "Try telling that to Mr. Claymore. Or the vet board. Or the cops."

I made a mistake. I flicked a glance at the phone on the wheel well.

Dax glanced over and saw it, and then his pretty-boy face contorted into rage. He advanced on me. "You think you're so smart? You're recording this?" I lifted the shovel, ready to use it as my own weapon, but he was too quick. He wrapped both his hands around my throat, causing me to drop the shovel and claw at his fingers.

I choked, breath cut off, desperate thoughts flying through my head. How I should've swung the shovel before he came in close. How I shouldn't have left Montana without talking to Levi.

Levi.

Fuck. I loved him. I loved him, and I'd fucked this up so badly.

Just then, a car came flying around the side of the stable and barely skidded to a stop. Right in front of us.

Dax was distracted by it and loosened his hold on my

throat, allowing me to take in a lungful of air. I was distracted because I saw through the windshield it was Levi. He wasn't a cowboy in a white hat riding in on a white horse.

No, he came to the rescue in a white sub-compact.

EVI

SOMEONE WAS CHOKING MY MATE.

I was going to kill the punk.

Charlie had been using a shovel, a fucking *shovel*, as protection, but it had been rendered useless. Some guy had both hands wrapped around her throat. At least he had until I pulled up. In the moment of distraction, Charlie wrenched herself free and grabbed the shovel again. I could see the marks on her neck from the assault, knew that if I hadn't arrived when I had, she'd be dead within seconds.

An animal-like snarl issued from my throat as I threw open the door.

She shouldn't be in a situation like this. Not her. She was meant to have her nails done, her clothes pressed crisp. Hell, cute little earrings in her ears. It looked as if she'd slept in her clothes, or maybe hadn't slept at all since she'd had to drive all night to be here. There was terror in her eyes. Shock, too.

She'd been on her own long enough. I'd take care of this fucker. With pleasure. My wolf was very pleased with the idea.

I shot from the car and ran for the guy. He had enough sense to recognize I was now a bigger threat than Charlie and her shovel. He was ballsy enough to keep a slick smile on his face although when I didn't slow down on my approach, it slipped.

I punched him in the face, and he went down hard. I was pleased to hear the sound of his nose breaking. Blood spurted down his chin.

"You messing with my mate?" I asked, my voice deep and gravelly. The only person I'd spoken to since I'd left Montana was the fucking rental car agent.

"Levi," Charlie gasped as she coughed and choked, trying to regain her breath. While she was standing, she was wobbling a bit. "What are you doing here?"

I took a deep breath and for once, for the first time in my fucking life, I smelled my mate. Sweet, bright like sunshine. The sharp tang of fear that accompanied it was what pissed me off. Nobody fucked with my mate. My wolf howled and growled at the same time. She was here with me but in danger.

"We've got some unsettled business, doll. Starting with this fucker." I pointed down at the asshole.

"This doesn't concern you." He scrambled to his feet, nose bleeding, and produced a knife from his pocket. He opened it and swiped at me with it. "You need to leave."

I wanted to laugh at the attempt to scare me. As if the knife would do me any kind of damage. "You think I'm asshole enough to walk away from a woman in danger?" I asked him. "*My* woman?"

He swiped again, his blade nearly connecting with my ribs, and I growled. It wouldn't matter if he cut me. My wolf had emerged when Rob had goaded and prodded it to come out. My shifter genes had surfaced, and I'd spontaneously heal. But Charlie... she was in danger. From this guy.

"You think I'm going to let *my* woman, *my* mate, be threatened? What's that you have there?" I indicated a cardboard box on the ground nearby. "Let me guess. Ketamine."

Charlie gasped. That little sound was all the proof, all the indication I needed to know I'd been right. Clint had put it together. It made sense, even though I hadn't wanted to admit it. All of it. Except for this fucker. She hadn't been doing it because she wanted to. She'd done it because she had to. No woman wanted to do things against her will or be forced to defend herself with a fucking manure shovel.

The guy looked at Charlie and shook his head. "You shouldn't have told. You're dead now." Spittle flew from his mouth in a rage. He charged—not for me, for Charlie again.

No fucking way. My mate was in danger. Mortal danger. I wasn't used to the intensity of feelings coursing through me at the split second vision of my mate being attacked. I was still trying to process it as my wolf took over. He snarled and between one blink of an eye and another, I shifted.

Then attacked.

Charlie raised her shovel as if to strike his arm, to knock his knife away but I flew through the air and sunk my wolf fangs in his forearm. The forward momentum took the asshole sideways and to the ground. Charlie fell back onto her butt.

He screamed because I didn't give him any mercy, the bite snapping one of his arm bones. I felt the crunch between my teeth. I released, then turned to look him in the eyes. He was the one who was scared now. That was the last thought he had because I went for his throat and finished him.

He'd been trying to kill Charlie. My mate. I would protect her, no matter what. Even if it meant her discovering what I really was... and risking her running away.

 HARLIE

Levi was a wolf.

A wolf.

A wolf.

Holy shit. He was a black wolf bigger than any dog I'd ever seen. With huge paws. Amber eyes. Big teeth. A bloody muzzle.

Dax's blood.

A wolf. I had no idea how long my brain was going to be stuck on that because in a million years, it wasn't something I would have ever guessed. Married, maybe. He was really a CIA agent. He had a kid. Any possible option but that because... a wolf.

He stood beside Dax's prone, unmoving body staring at me. Into me. Somehow, I saw Levi in the gaze, which was insane.

Maybe I'd been dosed with ketamine. It was known to

produce hallucinations. I'd just seen a guy, my lover—ex-lover—turn into a wolf and rip out Dax's throat.

I dropped the shovel handle and crawled across the ground toward Dax to see if I could help. I wasn't thrilled to have Dax blackmail me, but I hadn't wanted his throat ripped out either. I wasn't a human doctor, but I could—

Levi... *the wolf*, leaned into me, putting his weight into it, pushing me away from Dax. I didn't touch Dax, but I could see it was too late. Doctor or not, it was obvious. Blood pooled beneath his head and upper back. His gaze was fixed and up at the sky.

He was dead.

Levi had killed for me. To protect me because there was no doubt Dax had every intention of stabbing me.

I turned my frightened gaze on Levi. I wasn't scared of *him*, specifically, but he had just gone all Incredible Hulk and turned into a fucking animal. And I'd thought we'd bared all at the overlook the other day. But this? Yeah, he'd left this out. He licked my hand as if to comfort me.

"Levi?" I croaked. "Holy shit. You're... um, yeah."

He licked again. I buried my fingers into his thick fur and choked on a sob. And then I had my whole face buried against his soft neck, and I was bawling. Not for Dax. Well, maybe a little for Dax. But mostly releasing the trauma of the past month, since this whole ordeal with Dax began. Especially the last twenty-four hours, believing he was going to do something awful to Pops and then to me. Leaving Levi.

But he was here now. And he was a wolf. And oh, God, he'd just killed a man.

What had I done? What had I set into motion with my actions? "What am I going to do?"

The weird sound of bones and cartilage and other things I couldn't even process had me blinking past the tears and seeing Levi switch back from a wolf to... a huge naked guy. The guy I recognized. The one I knew every inch of... or thought I did.

Seeing the blood on his face made me gag. The very idea of killing someone with my teeth... I started laughing. I was definitely a touch hysterical because I was thinking I really did have a gag reflex after all.

"Are you all right?" Levi asked, stroking my hair back from my face, his touch so gentle in comparison to what I'd just witnessed.

He looked a mixture of rage-filled and worried.

"I'm not sure," I admitted truthfully. Was I all right? I glanced at Dax, swallowed. "This is bad. Levi, I killed a guy."

He shook his head. Hard. "No. You didn't kill him. You were defending yourself and then a wolf came out of nowhere and attacked."

I knew he was trying to make up some kind of story, but it wasn't a story because it *was* true.

Glancing around I popped up to my feet. "The cameras. Claymore has some out here." I searched the top corners of the stable beneath the eaves. I didn't see the black orbs like at the airports or in the ceilings at a store that my boss had installed around the outside of the property. Nothing since we were in the back where the only thing that usually happened was open and close a paddock gate or pile manure. We were at the far edge of the property, the land saved for open pasture where Seraphina was casually grazing. I exhaled in relief. Dax's trip to my office would have been seen, but he entered my office alone. "There aren't any back here."

Levi grabbed his tattered shirt, the one that had fallen off of him when he'd turned into a wolf and wiped his face. He went bare assed over to his car, leaned in and emptied a water bottle onto the shirt, then wiped his face and neck clean. When done, he tossed the sodden mass onto the ground. He grabbed for a small bag next, pulled out some clothes.

All the while, I stood there dumbly, staring. I was enthralled, but not aroused. God, how could I be? My lover was a wolf who was wiping another man's blood from his body.

This was nuts.

"Um, Levi... I think you might need to explain some things to me."

He looked my way as he tugged a pair of jeans up over his lean hips then zipped them up. "I'll tell you everything later. Now we've got to deal with this." He glanced at Dax.

I bit my lip. Lost. "Why... why are you helping me?"

He came over to me, cupped my face. All traces of Dax's blood were gone from his skin, and if I hadn't seen it, I wouldn't have believed he'd even done what he did. "Did you give this fucker ketamine to sell on the streets?"

I licked my lips, tipped up my chin. "Yes."

"How long has it been going on?"

"A month."

"Are you doing it for the money?"

I shook my head. "No. He was blackmailing me. I have proof. Oh, my phone. I recorded all of this to try to get out of it, to take to the police along with the ketamine I'd ordered. That's why he attacked me." He dropped his hands, and I dashed over to grab it from the trailer. I looked down at it, saw that it was still recording. Minutes and minutes of everything that had just happened.

"Delete it," Levi said, his voice calm and even.

I stared at him, mouth open and wide eyed. "I'm going to go to jail for murder."

"Do you think I'd let my mate go to jail? That I won't protect you from anything?" He glared at Dax even though he was dead.

"Mate?" I squeaked. I remembered the words Rob had used. Happy mate, happy fate. Oh God, they were all werewolves, weren't they? All of them knew. Had kept the secret.

"Yeah, mate, and I won't let anything happen to you." He tipped his chin toward my phone. "Deleted?"

I glanced down at the device, swiped my finger a few times. "Yes."

"Good girl. Now call the police."

My mouth fell open once again. Was my brain slow or was what he was asking so confusing? I couldn't keep up with what he was planning. "What? Why?"

"Call them. Tell them you came across a dead body. It looked as if he'd been attacked by an animal."

I blinked, processing.

"Make the call, doll. Everything's going to be fine. I promise."

29

EVI

IT TOOK two hours of questioning before the police allowed us to leave. They'd asked us all kinds of questions about what had happened, and we'd told the truth. Minus the blackmail. Charlie had called her boss, Mr. Claymore—I'd never found out his first name—right after the police, and he'd come down from his fancy mansion. He'd ensured Charlie was all right and waited with us for the police. Once the questioning started, he'd listened to every word. I saw how Charlie was a good fit for the very precise older man. He seemed as worried for Charlie. Thankfully, the guy wasn't an asshole. In fact, the opposite, more concerned about my mate than anything else. I had no doubt news would spread, but he didn't give a shit. That either made him a decent guy or rich enough to not care.

I'd told Charlie to stick to the facts, to tell as much truth as possible, which she'd done. While she was still shaken up, she'd given a thorough report. She'd just returned from Montana and had parked at the back of the stable to put Seraphina in the paddock after the long ride. She'd found Dax, her co-worker on the ground. Dead.

The medical examiner had taken one look and agreed with Charlie's professional opinion about an animal attack, possibly a wolf. They'd been seen up in the mountains and while unlikely, there was no other plausible explanation for what happened to Dax.

It wasn't as if they'd expected Charlie to be a wolf. The idea of anyone shifting into an animal was only something humans expected in fiction or the movies. Even if the police detective had been unconvinced, she had an alibi. She'd been seen in Montana the night before and had a credit card receipt for gas in Wyoming in the middle of the night. As for me, I'd been on a plane and had chased Charlie down because I was madly in love with her, and she'd left in such a huge hurry—her grandfather had been unwell, and she'd returned home in a rush to get to him—she hadn't said goodbye.

Charlie'd given me a wide eyed stare as I professed my love for her to the local police. Claymore had smiled. Yeah, he wasn't an asshole. Between that pussy-whipped statement and the fact that I was the sheriff in Cooper Valley, Montana, the detective was on my side.

The only thing Charlie had thought of was the box of ketamine that Dax had been holding. She'd told me it had to go back to her office, that it was supposed to be there, and she had a co-worker justify its presence. She'd given me a twenty second explanation that a coworker named Bob had believed she'd added an extra zero to the quantity by mistake. The vials would be put to use, but wouldn't need to have another shipment for a while.

The body had been taken away. Mr. Claymore told Charlie to take a few days off with her *man* while he dealt with everything else. It was his problem to deal with... not Charlie's. After all that, we'd been free to go. Since the truck belonged to Claymore, Charlie rode with me in the rental. Once we cleared the gates to the property, I pulled over.

"You okay, doll?" Since the vehicle was so tiny, Charlie was right there. Our shoulders practically brushed.

I saw her throat work as she swallowed. "I think so. How did you even find me?" she asked, a furrow creasing her brow.

"Clint had the info for your boss. For where you worked. I figured you'd have to show up because of Seraphina."

"How... how did you get here? I mean, didn't you stay in town last night? I haven't wrapped my head around what I saw, and I guess after that, it's possible that you can teleport or something, but... how?"

I gave her a smile, wishing I could fucking teleport. "Plane... and fate." There weren't a shit ton of flights out of Montana. I just happened to luck upon one in nearby Bozeman heading to Denver. Some people might call it luck, but it was definitely fate.

I'd been fucked for years, not ever being able to shift or scent a mate. But now... now it seemed as if I'd earned the chance to be with Charlie. Fate had intervened, so I could save her. To make her mine. Although fate was also a bitch because she'd cut it damned close. A few more seconds, and Dax would've strangled her dead. I'd have to live with that image for the rest of my life.

Still, I wasn't going to fuck with what fate had given me.

"I don't know where to go," I told her, not pulling out

onto the road. I'd used my cell's map directions to get to the place from the airport, but now I had no idea where we even were besides west of town.

She blinked, looked around. "Oh. We can go to my place. My grandfather's at a church thing for most of the day."

"Lead the way."

"Only if we talk. About you. *Stuff.*"

"About the fact that I'm a shifter?" I stated plainly.

She blinked. "Oh yeah."

30

HARLIE

LEVI PARKED IN THE DRIVEWAY. We didn't go inside. Instead, we took a walk to my neighborhood park and sat under one of the beech trees, our backs against the grey bark. Levi hadn't said anything the entire way, only held my hand in his big one. It was comforting and reassuring, but I really wanted a hug, something all encompassing, so I could feel him all around me. But not yet. We had serious things to talk about. I had no doubt he wanted answers from me, even though most of them had been made clear at Claymore's. But I had questions. Lots of them.

"How crazy is it that I picked a stuffed wolf at the county fair?" I asked inanely.

"Not crazy. It was fate."

I wasn't sure I believed in fate, but he was right. It certainly seemed like fate.

"Are you really a werewolf?" I blurted, my mind still stuttering on the facts that made no sense.

He set his hand on my thigh, gave it a little squeeze. "Shifter. Yes. But only because of you."

I frowned and turned my head to look at him. Our sides touched, we were that close. "What?"

"I was the product of a mixed-mating. A human with a shifter. I told you my grandparents hated my dad for marrying my mom. It's because he was a shifter. My mom was human, and they thought she was tainted. The match is still generally frowned upon in the shifter world. It even goes against shifter law in most packs, and that was the case in my dad's pack although the law hadn't been enforced in several generations. My parents mated, and I was born, and we were a happy little family until I hit adolescence."

I tensed, sensing the part of the story I wasn't going to like. I remembered he'd told me his parents had been murdered.

"I hadn't shifted for the first time yet. First shift usually comes on around puberty, but fourteen wasn't particularly late. Still, it got people in the pack talking. The gossip was that I might not be able to because my mom's blood had tainted me." He paused for a second. "See, the prejudice goes both ways. The more the talk got going, the more some radicals got riled up. There's a lot of anti-human sentiment in the shifter world, especially in the less educated populations, and to be honest, most of the shifter population falls into that category. We like to stay up in the hills or mountains where we can run free. That means there's a lot of isolation. And with isolation sometimes follows close-mindedness."

My skin prickled. They sounded like the kind of racist fucks I'd been afraid of my whole life.

Levi picked up my hand and squeezed it. "You've already guessed the outcome."

I nodded, a tight band closing around my throat.

"My parents were killed for their love. I'd been at school at the time, so I'd been spared. I was sent to live with my human grandparents in Seattle after that. Of course, they couldn't forgive the shifters responsible, or shifters in general for what happened. If my parents hadn't married... I lived with them for four years. They forbade me from ever shifting or showing any wolf tendencies. And it stuck. I never did in all that time. Or after. Not once."

My heart beat faster. "Until now?" I guessed.

He nodded. "This morning. The moment I found out you left. My wolf went nuts, and I spontaneously shifted for the first time in my life. And then again when you were in danger. Do you know why?"

My brain tried to connect dots, but I was missing too much information. "No?"

"You're my mate."

That word again. I'd heard him use it back at Mr. Claymore's.

"What does that mean?"

"Wolves mate for life, doll. One partner until death. And the human part of them doesn't pick that partner—their wolf does. A normal shifter would instantly recognize his mate by scent, but, see, I'd never shifted. I didn't have the ability. I didn't know you were my mate. All I knew was that we have mad chemistry. That I was happier when I was near you. That making you feel good became my calling."

My breath caught. His words were a balm on my frayed nerves. They were everything I needed to hear. They were what he hadn't said on that huge boulder. The secret he couldn't reveal that gave away his true feelings.

"You see, my human side picked you and fell in love without even knowing you were mine. It was truly fate."

A tear slipped out of the corner of my eye, and I let out a laugh as I brushed it away. He loved me. His wolf killed for me. "This is nuts."

Levi squeezed my hand again. "I know it's a lot to take in. But what you need to know is that I'm yours. I'm your man. Come thick or thin. I'll never leave you, never stray, never cheat, never stop protecting and providing for you. And that's not just a promise, it's biology. It's hard-wired into me as you saw with Dax. That doesn't mean I wouldn't honor your wishes if you told me to stay away, but—"

I shook my head, fresh tears of gratitude pricking my eyes. "No. I don't want you to stay away."

"I'm sorry about what happened with Dax. I swear to you, I'm not dangerous. It was only because your life was in danger. A kill or be killed response to protect my mate."

My head wobbled as I nodded. "I understand. I... honestly, I don't think I'm sorry."

"I don't think I am, either," he said, and yet, I felt the weight of his words. He didn't take ending a life lightly. Just as he wouldn't if he'd killed someone in the line of duty.

"Come to Montana," he pleaded. "Bring your grandfather. There are enough people on the ranch to make sure he won't wander off or hurt himself as his mental health deteriorates. He'd be totally safe. And if he needs more, Audrey's a doctor and will help with whatever he needs."

"But... we're human," I said. "I'm not a shifter. I don't have a wolf inside me. Pops doesn't either." I frowned. "That I know of. God, now I'm going to wonder if everyone's got a surprise wolf inside them."

"Doll, you'd know about your grandfather," he said, most likely trying to keep me going off on a mental tangent.

"Well, isn't that a problem? That I'm human. You just said some hate outsiders, hate humans."

"No," Levi said. "Not in our pack. Marina and Audrey are human. Willow's a half-breed like me. Clint's mate, Becky, is human, as well. That means the babies, Lizzie and Lily are, too. We all take care of each other. It's a good place."

I gave a watery laugh because he was right. Wolf Ranch was a good place. "You make it sound idyllic."

"Well, to me it was. That was where I landed after living with my grandparents and suppressing my wolf side. They took me in, gave me a job and a place in the pack. Made me part of the family. I love Wolf Ranch." He brushed the backs of my thumb with his. "But if you needed to stay here, then I'd move. You're more important than my pack. You're my life."

I covered my mouth with my free hand, shocked. "You'd give up your pack to live amongst humans? After what you went through with your grandparents?"

His throat bobbed as he swallowed, and I could tell the idea pained him. "To be with you? Yes. I can't be away from you. It's... impossible."

"Oh, Levi." I threw my arms around his neck and straddled his lap, dropping kisses across his broad face. "I would never ask that of you. I'll... we'll move to Montana."

It was crazy and impulsive. To think I could quit my job, pack up my grandfather and move to another state after knowing a man for one week.

But I would.

Nothing had ever felt so right in my life. I didn't need to talk myself into it. I didn't need a wolf inside me to tell me Levi was my mate. I knew it was my fate. *He was.*

"You will?" Levi's choked response made my heart sing. His eyes were watery, his smile soft, his touch gentle, his voice full of awe.

I nodded. "I will. If you meant it about Pops coming, too. He's non-negotiable."

"Of course, he'll come," Levi said instantly, without a moment's consideration. "You can set up a practice out there. Or stay at home and raise our pups. Whatever you want to do."

"Pups. You mean Shadow's puppies?"

He laughed. "No, our kids. We call babies pups."

"Pups." I repeated in awe. We would have shifter children. Or at least, mixed-species, like him. I was going to join a wolf pack.

This was definitely crazy.

And definitely the best thing that had ever happened to me.

Levi gripped my hips and pulled me over his bulging erection. "You keep wiggling on my lap like this, and I'm gonna put you in that stupid rental card and drive you straight back to Montana to start on those pups right now."

I smiled, instantly eager to start, or at least to practice. "I have a bedroom here."

I shrieked as I found myself being hoisted into the air. Levi somehow managed to stand up and keep me wrapped around his waist, and he refused to put me down, carrying me down the block back to my house.

I unlocked the door from my perch, and he carried me inside, following my directions to my bedroom. I toed off my shoes the moment we stepped inside.

"Don't think I'm not going to spank that ass of yours for leaving Montana without a word to me," he said when he dropped me on the bed and rolled me to my belly. He gave my butt a firm smack that still stung even through my jeans.

I sat up to face him. "I'm sorry about that. I really am. Dax called from my house to tell me I'd better get him the drugs or he'd hurt Pops. I just loaded up Seraphina and left."

His expression grew sober. "Fuck, Charlie. I wish I'd known. I wish I could kill him all over again."

"You can get past it? What I did?" My eyes burned. We'd talked about the elephant in the room. No, the *wolf* in the room, but not my illegal activities. "I mean with the ketamine? I broke the law."

"I'm past it," he promised. "I understand what he was doing to you. How you had no choice. I understand how you got blackmailed into it. It's over now."

"Promise?" I gripped his shirt and pulled him down on top of me.

"I promise," he said. His eyes took on an amber glow.

31

EVI

I'D FOUND Charlie magnetic before but nothing compared to being with her now that my wolf had come out. That it seemed that every secret we'd kept was now revealed. That there was nothing between us but the clothes on our bodies. I could barely hold back. I claimed her mouth like my life depended on it, grinding the bulge of my erection in the notch between her legs.

She moaned and clung to me, her short nails piercing my skin as she yanked me closer, undulated against me. Yeah, she was right there with me. I ripped open her blouse, sending the buttons scattering across the room.

"Levi!" she cried, but I didn't hear fear. Only surprise. Eagerness.

With one hand, I reached behind her to unhook her bra, humming softly when her pert brown nipples came into my sightline. "Fucking perfect," I announced, already moving to the button on her pants. I needed her naked. Stat.

I pulled off her jeans and panties all in one go, Charlie shifting and lifting her hips to help. My nostrils flared as I took in her cinnamon and sugar scent. My beautiful mate.

Mine. Fuck, the full scent of her, recognizing it and her as fully mine.

I stripped out of my clothes and climbed over her, trailing the tip of my tongue from her belly button to her breastbone.

I flicked my tongue over one taut nipple then the other.

"Levi." She pulled me down on top of her again, and we both gasped when my cock pushed against her sopping entrance. This was going to be a quickie. We were both frantic. Both needing to be as close to the other as possible.

"Is it okay if I go bareback?" I rasped, barely able to put words together. "Shifters are free of STDs, and I really want to take my chances on knocking you up." Besides, I hadn't packed any condoms. Unless she had a stash somewhere, that was the only option to get in her.

She only hesitated a moment, which didn't offend me. My mate was a thinker. Then she nodded. "I'm on the pill, so it probably won't happen."

If she wasn't ready for pups now, I'd respect that. Hell, we'd have tons of fun just practicing. But if she did want them soon, I'd help her flush those suckers down the toilet.

I rocked my hips, and the head of my cock slid in without any guidance. A homing missile finding its hot, wet target.

"Oh fates, you feel good," I groaned. My wolf was in heaven knowing our mate was beneath us, that she was wet and willing and receptive. I rocked into her slowly, trying to dial back the sexual aggression surging through me. The need to take her hard and rough consumed me.

A scent flooded my senses. Not hers.

Mine.

Oh fuck.

I reared back, stopping all motion. Touching the tip of my tongue to my canines, I found them extended like a fucking vampire's.

I'd told her what I was, but hadn't even thought about claiming her officially.

"Charlie," I gasped. "I forgot to tell you something."

She panted, looking up at me with hooded eyes. "What? You want to talk... now?" She rolled her hips sliding that tight pussy along my dick and making my teeth drip their serum.

"Hang on, beautiful. It's big."

"I know it's big. Just fuck me with it."

"Shit, stop talking like that. I'm only holding onto my control by a thread."

She blinked, and her eyes came into focus. She pushed up on her forearms. "What is it?"

"Male wolves... they mark their mates. We call it the mating bite. It embeds my scent into your skin to tell other wolves to stay away."

"Oh God." Her voice held amusement. "Well, wolves are a territorial species, I guess that makes sense."

"In a shifter female, it would heal instantly. But in a human... well, I'm scared I'm going to hurt you."

She frowned. "So you want to do it now? Mark me as yours?"

"It's less *want* and more *need*. And because my wolf is new to me, I don't want to lose control. I'm afraid the more I try to hold back, the more things could go wrong, you know what I mean?"

I had no doubt what I'd done to Dax had popped into her head too.

She sat up more, chewing her lip thoughtfully. "So how big of a bite are we talking about? Like all your teeth? Just the canines?"

"God, fuck, it's not like Dax. Just the canines. Here." I brushed a finger over the spot I wanted to make permanently mine. "It could leave a mark—a scar." My body shook from the effort of holding back, especially since my dick was buried deep. I doubted she even knew her pussy was clamping and releasing me in little pulses.

My vision had that sharpened quality. I could taste the serum in my mouth. I didn't dare bite her during orgasm, as was tradition. Better to mark her superficially now. Hopefully satisfy my wolf, so he didn't go nuts when we were having sex.

"On my neck, but...?"

"Are you scared? Please don't be afraid of me. I'm not going to rip your throat out. Fuck, doll, I'd never harm you." I pulled out, so she wouldn't be pinned by me, but the moment I did, she wrapped her legs around my back and pulled me back down.

"I'm not afraid," she whispered. "I just like the full agenda. You know, for my spreadsheets."

Despite my strain, I smiled. She was fucking adorable.

"Okay, the full agenda." I forced myself to take a slow breath to get my head on straight. "Not your neck. Bad idea. I'm going to nip you right here." I traced the pad of my index finger over the side of her left breast. "No one will see the scar but me." I lowered my head and licked the place I planned to bite.

A surge of need raced through me, and I thrust deep and forcefully.

Fuck.

I needed to do it now. Before I lost my head completely.

"You okay with this, Spreadsheets? You're not scared?"

She rocked her hips and took me deeper. Pulled my head down to her breast. "Do it, Levi."

I groaned and flicked my tongue over her nipple while my dick slowly stroked inside her channel. Then I shifted my mouth to the side and sank my teeth in.

The urge was to bite hard and deep. Thrust hard and deep. Yet to keep from puncturing too deeply, I channeled the urge into the fucking, nailing her again and again with brutal thrusts as I held my mouth still.

She came, calling out my name.

Unprepared for her orgasm, I lost control when her channel squeezed my dick. Somehow—thank fuck—I managed to disengage my teeth from her flesh as I pushed up onto my arms and fucked the living daylights out of her. The bed slammed against the wall, and I was glad her grandfather was at a church thing.

The room spun. I lost touch with reality. Who I was. Whether I was wolf or man.

All I knew was that when I came, the world was changed.

At least my world.

It would never, ever be the same.

"Fuck, Charlie. Fuck. You're mine now. Forever mine." I was still pushing into her, but with slower post-climax thrusts. A show of appreciation for being inside her. For coming inside her. For leaving my scent forever in her skin.

Her skin!

"Charlie, doll. Are you okay?" I lowered my head to lick

her wounds to promote a speedy healing. There was some blood—not a ton, thank fate.

She thrust her hips up and took me deeper. "I'm so good," she murmured, like she was totally blissed out. Hell, she looked blissed out. Hair in a messy dark halo around her head, dark skin flushed, eyes barely open.

My beautiful mate.

"You sure? You need a painkiller or anything?"

"Mm mm." She shook her head lazily. "Just a nap."

Sweet woman. Of course she needed a nap. She'd driven straight through the night.

I eased out of her and settled by her side, spooning around her protectively while she slept.

I could hardly believe this was my reality now. I had a mate to protect and provide for. This sweet female to warm my bed at night and light up my days. And she wanted to do it with me in Montana. At Wolf Ranch.

And I was going to savor every fucking second of it.

EPILOGUE

 HARLIE

HANDS WRAPPED around my waist from behind, making me gasp.

I spun about, then set my forehead on Levi's chest. "Shit, you scared me."

"Hi, doll." He kissed the top of my head, the gesture sweet. "Missed you."

Usually, Levi texted when he left town after a shift. It wasn't necessary, but I loved anticipating his return. Since that fateful day in Colorado, we'd been inseparable.

Mr. Claymore hadn't been surprised when I gave notice. Beneath his straitlaced exterior, he was a romantic and wanted me together with Levi. While I'd given two weeks, he'd let me leave after one, paying me in full and with a bonus. After the fact that I'd found Dax dead—his interpretation of what had happened—he'd thought I deserved a little something extra.

Pops had been eager to go to Montana. Levi had remained and helped us pack a moving truck to take some of our things. The house would sit vacant for a time. It didn't need to be sold right away, and I wanted to ensure Pops was truly happy to relocate before we committed with something so substantial. He'd bought that house with Nan forty years ago. I'd expected him to want to stay, to hold onto the memories, but he'd been the first one to pack.

That had been two months ago. Since then, we'd settled into the bunkhouse together, Pops moving into one of the bedrooms on the main floor, near Johnny's. Levi had put his foot down about sharing the top floor with anyone, and Pops had agreed. He, too, was a romantic and had wanted to give use some privacy.

As if a twenty-something shifter and a senior citizen living beneath us offered us much of that.

But we were a family. While Johnny had parents and siblings of his own, he'd taken to Pops and started calling him that right away.

Johnny wasn't the only one who watched out for Pops. Shadow was just that, Pops' shadow, following him everywhere. The puppies had all been weaned and adopted by different members of the pack. If there had been any decision over who'd keep the border collie, it had been changed by the dog herself. She'd adopted Pops, and they were inseparable.

To me, it was reassuring. Shadow was supposed to herd cattle and sheep but seemed to take to herding elderly humans, too.

It was Levi who took care of me, and I loved every second of it. I hadn't filled out a spreadsheet in weeks.

"I missed you, too. Why didn't you call?" I asked him.

He looked down at me with those blue eyes that held a

hint of mischief along with the constant happiness. "I've got news."

"Oh?"

"We talked about you opening up your own practice. Having it on this side of the mountains is smart."

"We've talked about this. There's not a place to have one."

He tapped my nose. "The Markle property."

I frowned. "The place two doors down? The guy who Willow had been watching?"

I didn't go into detail because he'd been a drug mule, and it hit a little too close to home. No one compared me to the guy, but still, it struck a raw nerve.

"Him. His property's been vacant since he died. His will's out of probate, and the bank is selling the place. I want to put an offer in. Make it ours."

My mouth fell open. "That place is huge. I've seen the house and stable from the road. It's been updated, and it's... huge. We can't afford that."

I loved the idea, the stable making a great vet office, especially for large animals. Levi could lease out stalls to locals who wanted a horse but didn't want to stable one. The house was lovely, and there was room for kids. Pups. But it was impossible.

He sighed, stroked my cheek. "I know we said no secrets, but... well, I'm rich."

"Huh?"

He sighed, hooked an arm about my shoulder. "You done in here?"

I was in the tack room, mending a broken bridle. I hadn't done any major vet work since Colorado, only taking care of the pups and checking on the ranch horses, and I was puttering around for now, helping out on the ranch where I could.

"Sure." I set the tool I'd forgotten I'd been even holding down on the table. Levi flicked the lightswitch off as we went by, then led me out into the early evening.

The sun was setting earlier and earlier, and the snap of fall was in the air. We'd even had a rogue storm come through the week before and dump several inches of heavy, wet snow. I didn't mind. Not the colder winter than I was used to or the end of the glorious summer weather. No, I had Levi to keep me warm at night.

Every night. To imagine I'd even left him to sleep in my own bed that night we'd first had sex... I'd been an idiot. I'd been content ever since to be with him in his small bunk house bedroom.

His words swirled in my head. He was rich? Why did he stay in the bunkhouse? Why was he working as sheriff if he didn't need the money? The sheriff election was less than two months away, and he'd officially put his name on the ballot. We'd decided—together—it was something he wanted to do. He was good for the community, Cooper Valley and the wolf pack.

"Doll, I can hear your mind working extra hard."

"Well, I handled the fact that you're part shifter pretty darn well, so you've got to give me a minute about this. What do you mean you're rich?"

"My grandparents had money. Lots of it. While they might have disliked me, a lot, I was their only living heir. I guess they could have left it all to a charity or something, but they left it to me."

We walked toward the bunk house. Pops had put a roast in the crock pot, and he and Johnny would have it all pulled together soon for dinner.

"When was this? Recently?" Had they just died, and he hadn't told me?

"When I was twenty. They died within months of each other. I haven't touched a dime of it. Haven't wanted to. Didn't need it. Still don't. But we talked about starting a family, and you want your practice, and I'd like to run my own stable. It's close to the pack and—"

I stopped, reached up and covered his mouth with my finger. "You don't have to convince me. I think the idea is great."

I knew his grandparents were nothing but bad memories for him, but perhaps using their money for something he wanted, for a way for us to make good memories, to raise a family in a way that was completely different than what Levi had gone through, might help.

"Fuck, I love you," he growled.

I grinned, and he kissed me. Tongue was involved, and a hand was on my ass.

"When you two lovebirds are ready, dinner's on the table."

We broke away at Pops' words, and we turned to look at him. He was standing in the open doorway, Shadow by his side. The scent of roast and baked bread filled the air.

He turned and went back inside, leaving the door open. "Think he'll want to move?"

"The place has a mother-in-law suite over the garage. He can stay here if he wants, for now, but when it's time, he can move in there. Whatever is best for him."

I sighed. "Fuck, I love you," I repeated.

He pulled the cuffs from his utility belt. "How about we take these for a spin later? I'm hungry for more than roast."

He leaned in and nipped my neck, growled.

"Hurry up! The gravy's getting cold," Pops shouted.

Levi lifted his head, and we laughed. We'd wanted family. We'd wanted... love.

We'd gotten it, and we were ready for it to last a lifetime.

————

Ready for more Wolf Ranch? Get Ruthless next!

PACK RULE #6: KEEP HUMANS AWAY FROM PACK LAND.

My alpha told me to get rid of her.
Make nice and find out if she'll sell her property.
Keep her from bringing more humans close to our land.
But before I've even met her, I catch her scent.
The moon's full and I have to follow it. I can't stop myself.
I run straight into human territory, onto her property.
Find her bathing naked in the moonlight and show her my wolf.
Now all bets are off.
My alpha may want her gone, but I need her to stay.
In fact, I'll do anything to make sure she never, *ever* leaves.

Read Ruthless!

NOTE FROM VANESSA & RENEE

Guess what? We've got some bonus content for you with Charlie and Levi. Yup, there's more!

Click here to read!

WANT FREE RENEE ROSE BOOKS?

Sign up for Renee Rose's newsletter and receive FREE BOOKS. In addition to the free stories, you will also get special pricing, exclusive previews and news of new releases.

https://www.subscribepage.com/alphastemp

GET A FREE VANESSA VALE BOOK!

Join Vanessa's mailing list to be the first to know of new releases, free books, special prices and other author giveaways.

http://freeromanceread.com

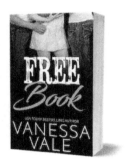

ALSO BY RENEE ROSE

Savage

Fierce

Ruthless

Bad Boy Alphas Series

Alpha's Temptation

Alpha's Danger

Alpha's Prize

Alpha's Challenge

Alpha's Obsession

Alpha's War

Alpha's Mission

Alpha's Sun

Shifter Fight Club

Alpha's Desire

Alpha's Bane

Alpha's Secret

Alpha's Prey

Midnight Doms

Alpha's Blood

Alpha Doms Series

The Alpha's Hunger

The Alpha's Promise

The Alpha's Punishment

Other Paranormal

The Winter Storm: An Ever After Chronicle

Sci-Fi

Zandian Masters Series

His Human Slave

His Human Prisoner

Training His Human

His Human Rebel

His Human Vessel

His Mate and Master

Zandian Pet

Their Zandian Mate

His Human Possession

Zandian Brides

Night of the Zandians

Bought by the Zandians

Mastered by the Zandians

Zandian Lights

Kept by the Zandian

Claimed by the Zandian

Other Sci-Fi

The Hand of Vengeance

Her Alien Masters

Regency

The Darlington Incident

Humbled

The Reddington Scandal

The Westerfield Affair

Pleasing the Colonel

Western

His Little Lapis

The Devil of Whiskey Row

The Outlaw's Bride

Medieval

Mercenary

Medieval Discipline

Lords and Ladies

The Knight's Prisoner

Betrothed

Held for Ransom

The Knight's Seduction

The Conquered Brides (5 book box set)

Renaissance

Renaissance Discipline

ABOUT RENEE ROSE

USA TODAY BESTSELLING AUTHOR RENEE ROSE loves a dominant, dirty-talking alpha hero! She's sold over a half million copies of steamy romance with varying levels of kink. Her books have been featured in USA Today's *Happily Ever After* and *Popsugar*. Named Eroticon USA's Next Top Erotic Author in 2013, she has also won *Spunky and Sassy's* Favorite Sci-Fi and Anthology author, *The Romance Reviews* Best Historical Romance, and *Spanking Romance Reviews'* Best Sci-fi, Paranormal, Historical, Erotic, Ageplay and favorite couple and author. She's hit the *USA Today* list five times with various anthologies.

Please follow her on:
Bookbub | Goodreads

Renee loves to connect with readers!
www.reneeroseromance.com
reneeroseauthor@gmail.com

ALSO BY VANESSA VALE

For the most up-to-date listing of my books:

Click here

or go to:

http://vanessavaleauthor.com/v/14s

All Vanessa Vale titles are available at Apple, Google, Kobo, Barnes & Noble, Amazon and other retailers worldwide.

ABOUT VANESSA VALE

Vanessa Vale is the *USA Today* bestselling author of sexy romance novels, including her popular Bridgewater historical series and hot contemporary romances. With over one million books sold, Vanessa writes about unapologetic bad boys who don't just fall in love, they fall hard. Her books are available worldwide in multiple languages in e-book, print, audio and even as an online game. When she's not writing, Vanessa savors the insanity of raising two boys and figuring out how many meals she can make with a pressure cooker. While she's not as skilled at social media as her kids, she loves to interact with readers.

Printed in Great Britain
by Amazon